Dirty Sexy Inked

NEW YORK TIMES BESTSELLING AUTHORS

Carly Phillips

Erika Wilde

SEXY

S E R I E S

CARLYPHILLIPS.COM
ERIKAWILDE.COM

"The love story Phillips and Wilde crafted was rare, dipped in a reality so natural and organic it held my heart from the very first page."
~ Audrey Carlan, #1 New York Times Bestselling Author

New York Times bestselling authors Carly Phillips and Erika Wilde bring you a dirty, sexy, smoking hot series featuring three bad boy brothers bonded by shocking secrets and their damaged past. Sinful, addicting, and unapologetically alpha, these men are every woman's erotic daydream . . . And your ultimate dirty fantasy.

Are you ready to get Inked?

Breaking hearts is what wild and rebellious Mason Kincaid does best. Hit it and quit it is his motto, and with his bad boy reputation and tattoos, he doesn't lack for female companionship. Until one hot night with the one woman he swore he'd never touch becomes an all consuming addiction he can't kick. Katrina Sands has been his best friend for years, but now that he knows what she feels like, and tastes like, there is no going back to being just friends. Hot, dirty sex has never felt so good . . . or so right.

* * *

This book is a work of fiction. Names, characters, places, and incidents either are products of the author's imagination or are used fictitiously. Any resemblance to actual events or locales or persons, living or dead, is entirely coincidental.

the jerk knew it, too, and didn't hesitate to use
m to his advantage.

I need you to put your seat belt on, please,"
 oh-so-sweetly as her hand gave his solid
a noticeable squeeze.

lutely. And call me Mason," he said as he
he belt around his waist, his tone as light and
 as the wink he gave the woman. "Since I'm
ass and you'll be servicing me, we might as
 a first-name basis."

a rolled her eyes, but the flight attendant
 his double meaning and gave him a blatant
 before moving on to the chairs in front of
re Clay and Samantha were seated. Straight
aisle from Mason was his youngest brother,
 with Tara, who was a bartender at Clay's
id's. The upgrade to first class had been
g, as were the individual hotel suites for
f them that awaited their check-in at the
tel.

ttendant walked down the rest of the aisle,
, Mason craned his neck to stare at her ass
ldn't see her anymore.

e glanced back at Katrina with one of his
sh grins and a shameless gleam in his eyes.
nk she'd be willing to induct me into the
b?" he asked, and Katrina knew he wasn't
easing.

owed her gaze in warning, because the
 of Mason banging some chick a few feet

Chapter One

"WE'RE OFF TO Las Vegas, Kitty-Kat," Mason
Kincaid said as he rubbed his hands together
in anticipation. "Sin City is the perfect place to get
down and dirty and have some fun. What kind of
trouble do you think we can get into while we're
there?"

Katrina Sands buckled her seat belt and settled
more comfortably in the first-class leather seat next to
Mason—her best friend since they were fourteen and
freshmen in high school. She wasn't at all surprised
that he was already making a mental list of all the wild
and reckless adventures that awaited him in a no-
holds-barred place like Las Vegas. Mason Kincaid was
a rule breaker, a thrill seeker, and a self-indulgent bad
boy who was all about pleasure and instant gratifica-
tion. From everything she'd heard about the city that
never slept, he'd be right in his element.

Oh, joy, she thought with a resigned sigh. It wasn't as though she was a prude. Far from it. She just wasn't thrilled about watching her best friend's man-whoring ways in action in Vegas. She spent enough time seeing it up close and personal on a day-to-day basis.

She turned her head and met Mason's bright blue gaze. "You do realize that this trip isn't all about you and your dick, right? That we're heading to Vegas because your brother Clay is marrying Samantha?" she asked, reminding him of that one important detail.

The corners of his mouth curved with an indulgent grin. "Of course I realize my brother is strapping on the old ball and chain tomorrow afternoon. But that doesn't mean the entire weekend is going to be all wedding, all the time. In fact, tonight Levi and I plan to take Clay out to make sure he spends his last evening as a bachelor in style."

Which gave Mason the perfect opportunity to carouse for a willing female to take back to his hotel room for the night. It's what Mason did. For as long as she'd known him, he'd had a hit-it-and-quit-it motto when it came to women, and he always made sure they knew the score up front. He didn't make promises or do commitment or anything longer than a one-time fling.

And each time Katrina watched it happen, a little bit of hope died inside of her. The hope that one day Mason would see her as more than just a best friend and the woman who managed to keep his personal and professional shit together. But the man was oblivious

to her deeper feelings for him
to tell him and risk certain
much easier, and safer, keepin
the friend zone.

She'd known him for tw
come to believe that Masor
ability to commit to any sir
wasn't hard for her to figur
kind of childhood he'd had
of and a mother who care
than her own kids. Mason
off a carefree, I-don't-give
was one of the few peopl
pain and resentment tha
masked.

The commercial plan
gas finished the boardi
cabin crew started closii
while another made a
electronic devices to air
flight attendant stopped
set her hand on his sho

He glanced up at h
complexion flushing a
male sex appeal her wa
breathtaking effect or
features, that sexy,
sleeves of bad boy ta
muscled arms, he
female gender.

And
that cha
"Sir,
she said
shoulder
"Abs
buckled t
flirtatious
in first cl
well be or
Katrin
laughed a
once-over
them, whe
across the
Levi, along
bar, Kinca
Clay's doin
each one o
Bellagio H
As the
hips swayin
until he cou
Then, h
typical wolf
"Do you th
mile-high cl
completely t
She narr
mere though

away from her wasn't something she cared to endure. "Don't even think about it."

He leaned in close so that his shoulder rubbed against hers and his lips were near her ear. "You're no fun, Kitty-Kat."

His warm breath stirred the purple-tipped ends of her blonde hair, and she barely managed to suppress the shiver of awareness tickling down her spine and causing her nipples to tighten uncomfortably.

"Having sex in a cramped bathroom in an airplane is not my idea of fun."

Jesus, maybe she *was* a prude, she thought with a frown. Or maybe it had just been too long since she'd indulged in sex of any kind. It had been nearly a year, and even that last time with the guy she'd been dating had left her unsatisfied and wanting.

"Things *could* get tight and hot," he agreed in a tone that was both amused and suggestive. "But that's not necessarily a bad thing."

She shook her head. "You're such a—"

"I know, I know," he said, cutting her off before she could finish. "I'm a manwhore."

He *was* a male slut, and he didn't even bother to deny it.

"But just for the record, you know I have way more fun than you." He settled back into his seat as the plane started moving away from the gate, his features suddenly turning serious as he studied her.

"What *have* you done for fun lately?" he asked, as if he believed she wasn't capable of having a good time.

"And for that matter, when was the last time you got laid?"

Her mouth dropped open at the unexpected question, and she snapped it shut again and glared. Screw him for being an asshole and *going there*.

He smirked. "Yeah, that's what I thought."

Her fingers itched to smack that smug look right off his face. "What the hell is *that* supposed to mean?"

"You've just been really uptight lately," he said with a shrug. "On edge and a little short and snappy with me."

Oh, yeah, the idiot was so damned obtuse. Her being *uptight* had everything to do with his womanizing and inability to see what was right in front of his face.

She was his best friend, and knew everything about his shitty past, his less-than-ideal childhood, and his abandonment issues. And though she'd proven over and over again that she wasn't going anywhere and would always be there for him, no matter her own personal demons and pain, he took her for granted, never seeing her as anything more than good old Kitty-Kat.

Then again, was it really his fault that she loved him with more than just friendship or sister-like affection? That he wasn't capable of returning those feelings for a variety of reasons—the main one being that he was emotionally damaged and didn't know how to let someone *intimately* close? No, she couldn't blame him. At least he was honest about who he was and what he was capable of.

It wasn't *his* fault she wanted more. It was hers, for holding out hope.

Maybe that was part of the problem, she thought as she searched on her phone for an audio book to listen to during the flight. It was so easy for Mason to take advantage of her always being around and at his beck and call. Hell, who was she kidding? She'd *made* it easy for him, and maybe it was time that she reevaluated her feelings for her best friend, and the fact that they weren't reciprocated.

Because there was one thing she knew for certain—unrequited love sucked big hairy balls.

He placed his hand on her bare arm, and her traitorous pulse sped up a few notches as she glanced at his strong forearm and the dark brown braided leather bracelet that was wrapped twice around his solid wrist. She'd given it to him for his most recent birthday, and it looked sexy as hell on him with all his tribal tattoos.

Ignoring the way her body warmed in all those neglected places, she lifted her gaze to his, and he gave her a playful smile.

"You know, maybe you ought to take advantage of Sin City, find some random guy who does it for you, and work out some of that tension you're carrying so you can loosen up and relax."

Katrina wasn't sure if he was joking or serious, but she bit back an irritable retort that would give way too much credence to his *uptight* opinion of her and instead dished it right back to him. "Yeah, maybe I'll do that," she replied enthusiastically.

Screwing a random stranger so wasn't her style, but *he* didn't need to know that.

He blinked at her in surprise. Clearly, he hadn't expected her to so readily agree to his indecent suggestion. That shock was quickly followed by a slight frown, as if he wasn't sure how he felt about her having a one-night stand, despite the fact that *he'd* brought it up.

Whatever, she thought as she tamped down her frustration.

Done talking, she glanced away from Mason, put her earbuds in, and closed her eyes as the plane raced down the runway and lifted off the ground. Her stomach dipped at the initial ascent, and she breathed slowly and deeply while coming to a very difficult decision. One she'd been struggling with for the past few months but that was suddenly becoming much too clear.

After the happy couple was married and they all returned from Vegas, Katrina needed to make life-altering changes. It was becoming increasingly hard and painful to be around Mason day in and day out and watch him go from one woman to another. It was time to reevaluate her life, as well as her job as manager of Mason's tattoo shop, Inked.

And that meant moving on from the one man she wanted but would never have beyond the friendship and the secrets that they shared.

✧　　✧　　✧

WHAT THE HELL? With a perplexed frown, Mason watched and *felt* Katrina's silent withdrawal from their conversation, and him, as she pushed in her earbuds, closed her eyes, and blocked him out in the process. One minute he'd been teasing her, and then the next, *bam*, he was being silently dismissed—this after she'd much too eagerly agreed to have a fling in Vegas.

Females, he thought with a shake of his head. God, he'd never understand them.

Okay, that statement wasn't entirely true. He had no problem relating to women when they were on their knees sucking his cock, or begging him to fuck them harder, faster. Hot, mindless sex and mutual pleasure—yeah, those things he had no problems comprehending. Hell, he understood *that* language without speaking a word.

But this increasing moodiness of Katrina's over the past few months? Jesus, he felt as though he were tiptoeing through a minefield, and he had no fucking idea how to deal with the situation, or her, without everything blowing up in his face.

Despite all the rough and terrible things she'd gone through in her life, she'd always managed to keep that shit buried deep inside and maintain an upbeat facade. She'd always been the one to make him smile on a bad day, or talk him out of a funk, or crack a joke when he, himself, was in a pissy mood.

Not so much lately.

So what the hell was going on with her? Katrina had never been one to show signs of PMS, so that theory was out. She wasn't in a relationship, so he didn't have to worry about some guy treating her badly. Then again, her irritation was always directed at him, and no one else. She was polite and cheerful with clients at Inked. She even joked around and teased the other employees in the shop, but when he attempted to join in on the fun, she shut him down and shut him out.

Just like now.

Jamming a hand through his hair in frustration, he glanced at her as the plane finally leveled out. Her eyes were still closed, giving him free rein to really take in her appearance. He loved her blonde hair that was tipped in purple and fell around her shoulders in soft waves. The funky style matched her unique personality, as did the clothes she wore. Today she was dressed in a pair of acid-wash jeans and a long gray tank shirt that was accented with black lace trim for a bit of an edge. The sleeveless top exposed the array of colorful butterfly tattoos covering her entire arm and all the way up the side of her neck.

Being a tattooist himself, he could honestly say that the female artist who had inked Katrina's skin had done a stunning job—with the artwork and tattoo itself, and for giving Katrina back her sense of self-worth. Mason was one of the few people who knew of the physical and emotional scars the intricate design concealed, and he often wished that *he'd* been the one to lay that ink on her instead.

His gaze traveled back up to her face, leisurely taking in her delicate features—the sweep of her long, dark lashes, her cute, pert nose, all that creamy skin, and those soft, full lips that were made to cushion a man's cock.

Yeah, he fucking went there.

He swallowed back a groan as a blast of heat and the secret desire he harbored for his best friend made his dick twitch with awareness. It certainly wasn't the first time he'd thought of Katrina in a sexual way. Hell, she'd flip out if she knew that she was his go-to fantasy when he woke up in the morning with a hard-on and wrapped his fingers around his cock. As he stroked himself, all it took were erotic mental images of her moaning and arching beneath him as he sank deep inside of her tight, slick flesh to get him off every single time, and quickly, too.

He was a goddamn pervert for thinking of her that way. She was his *best friend*, for crying out loud, and there was no way he'd ever fuck that up with sex. Ever. Katrina meant way too much to him to ever cross that line, no matter how much his dick protested his decision. She was his rock, the one person he always knew he could depend on to be there for him, no matter what. She knew things about him that no one else did and accepted him despite his flaws and weaknesses.

Most importantly, she was the one and only woman he'd ever trusted—*fucking mommy issues*, he thought bitterly—and he'd never do anything to jeopardize what the two of them had been through together, and what they shared as *best friends*.

Which was why her odd behavior lately piqued his concern, and he certainly didn't like how it felt as though she was distancing herself from him. Something was definitely off, and he had to admit that the thought of losing Katrina in any capacity scared the shit out of him.

He rubbed his clammy palms down his jean-clad thighs, hating the uncertainties that were growing stronger and stronger with each passing day. He didn't want to panic, but something was up with Katrina, and the fact that he couldn't pinpoint the issue was driving him nuts. When they returned from this trip, he planned on finding out what, exactly, was causing her mood swing.

Being in first class, the passengers had their own attendant, and Mason turned his attention to the woman who'd flirted with him earlier, who was now taking refreshment orders and working her way down the aisle toward his row.

When she reached him, he read her name tag—Tawny—as she gave him an inviting smile. "So, Mason, here I am, at your service," she said, taking her cue from his earlier flirtatious comment. "What can I get for you?"

He didn't miss the way she'd deliberately left out the words *to drink*. Oh, yeah, she was definitely playing his kind of game, and since Katrina was giving him the cold shoulder, he welcomed the distraction. "What would you recommend, Tawny?"

She licked her glossy lips, her brown eyes all but eating him up. "What I'd *like* to recommend isn't on the airline's menu."

He chuckled, recognizing an overture when he heard one. "In that case, I'll take a Sprite . . . for now."

She wrote his order on her note pad, then glanced past him to Katrina—who was oblivious to everything except what she was listening to through her earbuds, her eyes still closed. "Would your girlfriend care for anything?" Tawny asked with a curious raise of her brow.

Girlfriend. The word was so foreign to him, not just in terms of Katrina, but because he'd never stayed with a woman long enough to get romantically or intimately involved beyond sex, which was what that word implied. But he knew what Tawny was getting at, even if she didn't seem overly concerned if he *was* taken.

"She's not my girlfriend," he assured the pretty flight attendant, though with Katrina sitting by his side, he felt an odd and unexpected moment of regret that made absolutely no fucking sense to him.

Tawny grinned at him. "That's good to know."

"I'm not sure what she wants, so I'll have her press the service button when she wakes up." Or whatever Katrina was doing. She'd been the one to blatantly ignore him, and he wasn't about to disturb her and risk rousing the shrew again.

Tawny turned to Levi and Tara and took their drink orders, too, then headed back toward the galley at the front of the plane. A few minutes later, she appeared again holding a tray with everyone's drinks, and starting with the first row, she passed out the refreshments until she reached Mason again.

She placed a note on his tray and tapped it with her finger, drawing his gaze to the digits she'd written on the piece of paper. "I'm laid over in Vegas for the weekend, so if you're up for some fun, give me a call."

"I might just do that," he replied with a wink. He was certain that, after the wedding tomorrow afternoon, he'd have plenty of free time on his hands, and it was nice to have a sure thing lined up.

Once she was gone, Mason lifted the note so Levi could see the phone number and gave his brother a smirk. "I haven't even gotten to Vegas and I've already scored."

Levi rolled his eyes. "Seriously, dude?"

"I can't help it if women want me," Mason said with a shrug. "No need to be jealous just because I get laid on a regular basis."

"You're such a cocky bastard, and I'm far from jealous," Levi replied, his always serious tone tinged with humor. "It's called being *discriminate*, not that I expect you to understand what a big word like that means."

"Ha ha. It means you're boring as fuck." He couldn't resist goading his by-the-book, rule-abiding, straight-laced cop brother. While Mason had been a hell-raiser and defiant during his teen years—and still had his moments of being wild and impulsive—Levi had been a quiet kid who'd been much too serious and never gotten into trouble. He thought about consequences before he acted, he never drank alcohol, and he obviously didn't let his dick lead him astray.

Which meant Levi missed out on a whole lot of fun, and wasn't that the point of going to Vegas? Other than his brother getting hitched, of course.

"Are you going to be a Debbie Downer on this trip?" he asked Levi.

His brother drank the last of his orange juice before responding. "Just because I don't chase after everything in a skirt like you do doesn't mean I'm a Debbie Downer."

Mason decided to test that theory. "So, that means you're up to taking Clay to a strip club for his last night as a free man?"

Before Levi could reply, Clay leaned over the armrest, his head popping into the aisle as he jumped into the conversation he'd obviously been listening to. "Sorry to disappoint you, Mase, but we're *not* going to a strip club."

Mason threw his hands up in the air, disappointed in both of his brothers. "See, now *this* is why I don't do serious relationships. Being pussy-whipped just sucks all the fun out of what a true bachelor party should be."

Chapter Two

A FTER ARRIVING IN Vegas and checking into their individual suites at the Bellagio, the guys and girls split up to go their separate ways for the afternoon and evening. While Mason promised to make Clay's last day and night as a free man a memorable one, Katrina and Tara opted for a more low-key approach for the bride-to-be and took Samantha to the hotel spa, where they all indulged in long, luxurious massages, body wraps that left their skin soft and glowing, and hydrating facials.

A few hours later, nails complete, they sat side by side in pedicure chairs, their final treatment of the day. All three of them were wrapped up in soft, fluffy robes, drinking a glass of champagne, and eating chocolate-covered strawberries.

Life didn't get much sweeter than this, Katrina thought with a content sigh. She settled back in the cushy leather chair while enjoying her first ever detoxifying foot soak, unable to recall ever being so pampered and relaxed or feeling so calm. Since sex wasn't in her foreseeable future, despite what she'd told Mason today on the plane about hooking up with a random stranger, she decided that nurturing her body, mind, and soul with an array of therapeutic services was the next best thing.

"Thank you for an amazing day," Samantha said, her smooth complexion glowing from her recent facial, and for the man she was about to marry. "I can't tell you how much it means to me to have you two here for the wedding this weekend, and for standing up as my maids of honor. I adore you both so much."

Katrina smiled. Samantha might have come from a wealthy family, but she was sweet, genuine, and the best thing that had ever happened to Clay. "We feel the same way about you," she said as the three of them clinked their champagne glasses together in a toast.

"And we wouldn't miss this wedding for anything," Tara added as she picked up a ripe, red strawberry and bit into the chocolate tip.

Samantha raised a recently shaped brow. "Why, because you can't believe that Clay is really getting married and want to witness it for yourselves?" Her tone was light and teasing, her pretty blue eyes sparkling happily.

Katrina knew she was joking, but wanted the other woman to know that their reasons for being here were much more authentic. "No, because you and Clay are meant to be together, and we're all family, which means we'll always be here for you."

The word *family* didn't come easily to Katrina, not when her own deadbeat father had walked away when she was thirteen, and her mother had turned around and remarried a man who creeped Katrina out—and for good reason, she'd eventually learned. The people she now considered family were Mason and his brothers, and the few others who were allowed into her inner circle. People who had proven themselves loyal, dependable, and trustworthy. And now, that small group included Samantha.

"If we're family," Samantha said, looking from Katrina to Tara with affection. "Then that makes you two my sisters, which I've always wanted to have."

Katrina smiled as she wriggled her toes in the warm, silky water bubbling around her feet and ankles. "That's good, because you're stuck with us."

Quiet moments passed as the three of them finished their champagne, and the calluses around their heels and toes were exfoliated, followed by hot towels around their calves and a paraffin wax treatment that left their feet smooth and soft to the touch. Samantha bought a pretty pink nail polish she wanted each of them to wear, which matched the color of the maid-of-honor dresses and the flowers in her bouquet for tomorrow's wedding.

"So, what would you like to do on your last night as a single woman?" Tara asked as they waited for their toenails to dry. "I've heard Thunder From Down Under is the show of choice for bachelorettes. Watching hot, chiseled men dance and strip and thrust their hips could be fun."

Samantha wrinkled her nose in a clear veto of that idea. "I'll pass on the Aussies. The only man I want to watch strip naked is Clay. That man is so freakin' hot I'd give *him* a lap dance any day," she said with a cute, champagne-induced giggle.

Yeah, Samantha was head-over-heels in love, and Katrina couldn't help but envy the fact that her friend had found *the one*—and Clay was equally smitten. Their unwavering relationship and feelings for each other made Katrina all the more aware of her own lack of male companionship, and made her wish for *more*.

Even though she'd harbored more intimate feelings for Mason for years, she'd tried to give other men a chance. She'd even been in a few short-term but committed relationships with nice, decent guys. Safe men who didn't intimidate her and treated her with the kind of respect a woman deserved. Easygoing men who didn't judge her by her purple-tipped hair, her eccentric clothing, or her sleeve of butterfly tattoos that made others label her as white trash or a tramp— terms her own stepfather had used to degrade and humiliate her.

But deep inside, Katrina knew that focusing on those more passive qualities when it came to the men she'd dated had been part of the problem and why those attempts at a relationship hadn't worked for her.

She wanted that safety and trust and respect—what girl didn't?—but she also yearned for intense passion and the kind of heated desire that overwhelmed her body and senses. She wanted a man who was confident in his ability to take control and introduce her to the kind of forbidden pleasures her body craved, without making her feel cheap or dirty or vulnerable afterward.

So far, she hadn't met a man with that unique ability, and maybe she never would. Which meant she'd eventually have to settle for a man who made her feel appreciated and secure, and forgo her fantasies of hot, demanding sex.

Samantha's phone pinged, and she picked it up, then swiped her finger across the screen to unlock it. A dreamy smile curved her lips. "Speaking of my future hubby, he just sent me a text."

"What are they up to? No good?" Katrina asked curiously, because the boys hadn't revealed their plans for Clay before they'd gone their separate ways, and with Mason in charge of entertainment, there was no telling where he'd dragged his brothers off to.

"Actually, the three of them rented desert racers and went off-roading just outside of Vegas for the afternoon," Samantha said, sounding surprised.

Tara shook her head and finished the last of her champagne. "Boys and their toys and need for speed, right?"

Samantha typed out a reply to Clay's text. "At least they're staying out of trouble, which is more than I expected with Mason organizing all the activities." Her tone was wry as she mimicked Katrina's thoughts exactly.

"He's actually showing some restraint, considering all the raunchy adult shows in Vegas," she said, impressed.

"Right?" Samantha agreed in amusement as she read another message that pinged on her phone. "Now they're off to the Stratosphere Tower to go on some kind of thrill ride called Insanity that swings riders out and over the side of the hotel. From the *top* of the tower." Her tone rose in pitch as she read that last part.

Katrina didn't even bother to suppress a shudder at the thought of dangling over the side of a hotel. "They're such adrenaline junkies."

"If anything happens to Clay, I will personally kill Mason," Samantha said, and Katrina knew she wasn't kidding. "And after that, they're going indoor skydiving, then dinner."

"And what about us?" Tara asked.

"No way am I doing something so crazy," Samantha said adamantly. "In case you've forgotten, Clay calls me cupcake because I'm a lightweight and have a weak stomach, even without alcohol."

"I meant, what are *we* going to do," Tara clarified with a laugh. "If naked men are off the menu, how do you want to spent the rest of the evening?"

Samantha gave Tara's question serious consideration, and after a few minutes, her face lit up with excitement. "I know what I want to do! Last weekend I was watching the movie *Coyote Ugly* on cable, where they dance on the bar tops and get rowdy. It looks fun, and I know they have one of the franchises here in Vegas a few hotels down from the Bellagio. What do you two think? Want to go?"

"Sounds good to me," Tara said with an enthusiastic nod.

Katrina shrugged, up for anything that didn't include speed or heights. Indulging in a few drinks and dancing, even with just the girls, sounded like a fun way to spend the evening. "I'm game."

With their evening agenda settled, the three of them finished at the spa, then headed up to their individual suites to change and do their makeup and hair. Wanting to feel sexy for their night out, Katrina decided on a pair of slim black leather pants that rode low on her hips and a dark purple bustier that displayed her armful of tattoos. The front of the top laced up tight, and the snug bodice lifted and shaped her breasts so a bra wasn't necessary. She finished off the look with a stack of silver bangles on her bare arm and a pair of strappy high heels.

She tucked her room key and credit card into the front pocket of her pants so she didn't have to worry about a purse, and an hour and a half after parting ways to get ready, the three of them met up again. They grabbed a quick dinner, then walked the short distance to the New York New York Hotel, where Coyote Ugly was located, which also gave them the opportunity to take in the excitement and energy of the Las Vegas Strip.

By the time they arrived at the establishment that looked just like the iconic bar in the classic movie, the place was packed and rocking from the late 1990s music blaring out of the jukebox in the corner. There weren't any traditional booths or chairs, just standing-style tables on the outskirt of the dance floor, which was filled with men and women having a great time. Other female patrons were dancing on the bar counter, and guys were crowded around, egging them on.

Katrina led the way to one of the standing tables so they could order a drink, assess the situation, and watch the entertainment at the main bar before they decided what they wanted to do. Tara and Samantha followed her through the crowd, and by the time they reached a vacant table, Samantha was on her phone, tapping out a text. Judging by the smile on her face, Katrina assumed she was touching base with Clay. When a bar waitress came by, she ordered a round of shots for the three of them.

Samantha finished up her texting and slipped her phone into her cross-body purse. A few minutes later, their drinks were delivered, and Katrina raised her small glass to her two friends.

"To our first official girls' night out, even if it is on the eve of your wedding," she said in a loud voice to be heard above the noise level. "When we get back home, I think we need to do this more often, just the three of us. No men."

"Agreed," Samantha and Tara said at the same time.

They tapped their shot glasses together and swallowed the liquor in one gulp. It wasn't enough alcohol to get them drunk—no way did Katrina want to explain to Clay that his bride had a hangover on their wedding day—but it was just enough to warm her insides and loosen and relax her body.

A good-looking guy came up to Tara and asked her to dance, and with a little finger wave at her and Samantha, she followed him out onto the dance floor. Samantha and Katrina watched for a while, both of them dancing where they were standing at the table along the far wall.

After a while, another guy approached them, this one big and burly, rough around the edges, and clearly well on his way to being drunk. When he grabbed Katrina's hand to pull her away without asking if she wanted to dance with him, she yanked her arm back and gave him a sharp look that hopefully conveyed her feelings and made it clear she wasn't interested.

His narrowed gaze slid down the length of her in the kind of leer that made her stomach roil. Then he puffed out his wide chest and flexed his biceps as if he were trying to make up for the fact that he'd just been rejected. "What's the matter? I'm not good enough for you?"

And this was why she didn't go to bars. Hell, she rarely went to Kincaid's on their busy nights because she hated dealing with egotistical men who looked at her like an easy conquest. Instead of provoking him further, she gave the guy a sweet smile and said, "I don't dance with strangers."

It was a ridiculous statement considering that's what most people did in a nightclub, but her comment was so worth it when he frowned in confusion at her, as if she'd just given him a puzzle to figure out. Then he shook his head and slid his gaze to Samantha. There was no way Katrina was letting this guy even think about taking one step toward her.

"She doesn't dance with strangers, either," Katrina said just as the lug opened his mouth to say something.

After giving Katrina an irritated look, he turned around and finally left them alone.

Samantha laughed, her blue eyes full of playful mischief as she leaned closer to Katrina. "So, since we don't dance with strangers, want to dance with each other?"

Considering Samantha wasn't going to dance with any guy in the place and Katrina wanted her to have a good time, she nodded and the two of them joined the crush of people getting down to R.E.M.'s "Losing My Religion." Even though she didn't do it often, Katrina loved to dance, loved the sensuality of her movements and the way the beat of the music made her body come alive.

The two of them danced a few songs until Katrina lost track of time. But they were having fun as they laughed and watched other couples bust out trendsetting dance moves, and Katrina found herself envious of the females who were brave enough to get up on the bar top and dance in front of everyone.

She had no idea how much time had passed, but when she saw Samantha's gaze move to someone behind Katrina and watched her face light up like a woman in love, she wasn't surprised to see that the person she was beaming at turned out to be Clay, who had somehow found his fiancée in the crowd. *Jesus, had Clay put a tracking device on Samantha?*

Katrina leaned closed to Samantha so she could speak directly in her ear and be heard over the music. "What is Clay doing here?"

When she moved back, Samantha's expression was sheepish, and a tad apologetic. "I told him where we were and asked him and the boys to come join us."

Which meant that Mason was here, as well. Fucking fabulous, Katrina thought, not at all happy that *the boys* had just crashed their girls' night out and fun. Then again, it was hard to be upset with Samantha when all she wanted was to be with her man, but Katrina had expected it to be a Mason-free evening.

"Sorry to cut in and steal away my beautiful fiancée," Clay said as he wrapped his arms around Samantha and pulled her close.

The sinful gleam in his eyes told Katrina he wasn't the least bit sorry to be able to spend extra time with his bride-to-be before they went to their individual suites for the night.

"Last I saw, Levi and Mason were getting a beer

and heading over to one of those tables with Tara," Clay went on, jerking his head in the direction where the girls had been earlier. "I'm sure if you ask Mason, he'll dance with you."

Oh, hell no. That was one activity she'd avoided at all costs with Mason throughout the years, knowing that it would be sheer torture for her to have his hard, muscled body pressed so close, and to feel the grind of his hips against hers like a slow, sexual tease. And that's all it ever would be, since Mason wasn't attracted to her in the same way she was to him.

She made her way back to the area with tables and found Levi and Tara at one of them, both drinking a beer. No Mason, of course.

"Where's Mase?" she asked, knowing it was a bad idea even before she spoke, and that she wouldn't like the answer.

"Doing what he does best," Levi said, his tone droll, leaving no doubt in Katrina's mind as to what he meant. *Man-whoring.*

"He's over there by the bar, trying to charm his way into that girl's pants," Tara added unnecessarily as she pushed her long, dark hair over her shoulder. "Let's hope he doesn't drag her into the bathroom and get himself arrested in Vegas," she said with a snort.

Don't look, don't look, don't look. . . you'll just get upset over something you can't change, Katrina's subconscious warned her.

Like an idiot, she glanced over her shoulder and *looked*, her stomach in knots even before her gaze zeroed in on the one man who had way too much power over her emotions. It was a scene she'd witnessed so many times before—hot, gorgeous, tattooed Mason flirting with some random girl who had caught his eye, his devastatingly sexy smile promising the kind of pleasure most women couldn't resist. Judging by the way the pretty girl put her hand on his arm and swayed toward him so their bodies brushed, he was close to sealing the deal.

Hurt and anger warred within Katrina, the latter of which she had no right to feel. Logically she knew Mason was free to do what he wanted, with whomever he chose, but what upset her the most was the fact that he'd managed to ruin the fun she'd been having. He'd crashed their party, and she resented him being there and forcing her to watch him most likely leave the place with another woman.

She exhaled a deep breath, trying to release the ache tightening in her chest, but the tension remained, especially when she added in the fact that he'd called her *uptight* earlier today and accused her of not being able to loosen up and have fun. During that plane ride, he'd suggested she find a random guy to have a fling with, and in a moment of frustration, she'd told Mason that she would.

She remembered that dumbfounded look on his face, and his shock that she'd actually agreed to do something so out of character. She'd given him that flippant reply because he'd provoked her, but now she seriously considered putting herself out there to see what would happen, and how Mason would react.

And hell, maybe she'd get lucky tonight, too.

The Coyote Ugly bartenders were urging women to dance up on the counter, and Katrina realized that it was the perfect opportunity to show Mason that she was fully capable of letting loose and having a good time *without him*. She was finished standing on the sidelines, waiting and pining for something that wasn't going to happen because Mason didn't reciprocate her feelings.

You can do this, her inner vixen coaxed, bolstering her courage and confidence. *Get up on that bar and give Mason a show he'll never forget*.

And that's exactly what she intended to do, Katrina vowed as she headed for the stairs that led up to the staged bar, just as Don Henley's "All She Wants To Do Is Dance" started to play.

Chapter Three

ONE MINUTE MASON was trying to figure out how to nicely extricate himself from the overly aggressive woman who'd seemingly staked a claim on him the moment he'd walked into Coyote Ugly, and the next he was distracted by a round of loud cheers, appreciative male whistles, and catcalling coming from the direction of one of the bars.

Mildly curious as to what had the crowd all worked up, he glanced over the woman's shoulder toward the commotion. Every muscle in his body tensed when he saw *Katrina* dancing on top of the bar, looking hotter and more seductive than he'd ever seen her before. He'd also never seen her so . . . *uninhibited*, and especially in a public place.

What the fucking hell?

A combination of shock and awe held Mason's gaze hostage, and his mouth went dry as dust as he watched her body move so sensually to the beat of the music. Those small hips circled and swayed with lithe grace, and her cloud of gorgeous blonde hair cascaded down her back as she tipped her head, raised her arms above her head, and drove the men around her wild with a shimmying move that nearly brought Mason to his knees right where he was standing.

Lust made his blood surge like molten lava in his veins, spilling through him in a rush of carnal hunger. He couldn't move. He couldn't breathe. He could only stare at this bold, brazen, uninhibited woman he barely recognized as his *best friend*.

Who was this girl flaunting herself and what had she done with his composed and reserved Kitty-Kat?

The tight leather pants she wore molded to her sexy curves and her perfect ass—the same luscious ass she was currently putting on display as she bent over and ran a hand up her leg in a slow, sultry caress as she straightened once again. When she lifted her smoky gaze, Mason could have sworn that she was looking directly at him with those dark, come-hither eyes. Teasing *him*. Taunting *him*. Tormenting *him* with what he couldn't have. *Fuck*.

Or maybe his wild imagination was just playing tricks on him, because she'd never, ever given him any indication that she wanted to get down and dirty with him. Then again, this racy performance could be for another man entirely, and why did *that* thought make his stomach feel as though he'd just swallowed a dozen burning coals?

Hips gyrating to the music, she continued to skim those mesmerizing hands over her stomach and cupped her breasts over the corset top that was held together with just the thin ties that laced up the front. *So fucking naughty.* Her lips parted, and a hint of a smile played across her sinful mouth.

A mouth he suddenly wanted to do filthy, wicked things to. *Right now.*

Another ovation of rambunctious cheers attracted even more male attention to Katrina. Some guy offered her up a shot, and she took the glass and tossed back the liquor in one gulp, then sent a defiant glance in his general direction before continuing with her dirty dancing.

Jesus Christ, was she drunk? It was the only thing that made sense to Mason. Katrina wasn't an attention seeker, and she wasn't the kind of woman who paraded herself in front of men. Then again, nothing about her behavior lately had been predictable or typical, and this little display of rebellion was the last straw. He'd had enough. *Tonight*, he was going to find out what the hell was going on with her.

Before he could figure out a way to get Katrina out of there without causing a scene, one of the guys at the bar made the huge mistake of reaching out and touching her. The dickhead curled his hand around her calf and started sliding it upward, and Mason thought he was going to flip his shit.

He saw bright red, as hot, fierce jealousy jolted through him. An unprecedented depth of emotion flooded him as he pushed his way through all her admirers to make his way up to the bar. He told himself he was being a friend and protecting her from one of these douchebags who might take advantage of her being drunk, but that didn't explain the possessive feeling pumping through him with each step he took toward her. Add to that the steady stream of adrenaline ramping him up, and it was a potent combination that had him on edge and itching for a fight.

Realizing that the mob around the bar was too crammed and it would take him too goddamn long to get to Katrina, he instead went for the stairs that led directly to the top of the bar. As he climbed up, she caught sight of him and her eyes grew wide with panic, as if she realized she'd provoked him a little too far. He narrowed his gaze ominously, conveying his thoughts with that one look. *That's right, Kitty-Kat. Be afraid. Be very afraid because tonight we're finally going to hash out what the fuck your problem is.*

Now that Mason was on top of the bar—*and yeah, he knew men weren't allowed up there, but tough shit*—their audience grew. Heads turned their way as everyone watched the scene about to unfold. Despite how pissed he was, Mason was determined to set aside his anger and be nice and gentle about getting Katrina out of there.

When he reached her, he circled his fingers loosely around her wrist to make sure she obeyed. "Come on, Katrina, we're leaving."

She yanked her hand out of his grasp and lifted her

chin stubbornly. Her face was flushed and her eyes flashed fire. "I'm not going *anywhere* with you."

Okay . . . Apparently, he needed to line up a Plan B.

"Yes, you are," he said firmly, all too aware of all the eyes on them. "I suggest you come with me willingly, or you're not going to like the alternative. The choice is yours."

She crossed her arms over her chest, a reckless glint in her eyes as she glared at him. "You're such an asshole, Mase."

Clearly, she was mad at him. For ruining her fun? Or something else? That was the problem lately—he had no fucking clue what he'd done wrong. Since she was already furious, he figured things couldn't get much worse.

He sighed. "Since you think I'm an asshole, I might as well live up to my reputation." Before she realized his intent, he bent low, wrapped his arms around the backs of her thighs, and hefted her over his shoulder in a fireman's hold. She was slim and light— he bench-pressed more than what she weighed—and he heard her gasp at being taken by surprise.

She wriggled and squirmed as he headed back toward the stairs, with the crowd now cheering *him* on.

Her fists pummeled his backside. "Goddamn it, Mason Kincaid, let me down!"

He had no intentions of putting her feet back on the ground, because he knew he wouldn't get this kind of leverage over her again. "Not gonna happen, Kitty-Kat, so relax and enjoy the ride."

"Fuck you!" she bellowed.

He shook his head in disbelief. Jesus, when had she become such a goddamn hellcat?

He reached the bottom of the stairs and encountered Clay, who was frowning at him in that reprimanding way of his, and Mason knew that his big brother was going to be all . . . well, big brotherly, and try to interfere.

Before Clay could say a word, Mason spoke first. "Don't you fucking dare try to stop me. Katrina and I have some things to hash out, and it's happening *tonight*."

Surprisingly, Clay backed down, nodded in understanding, and let him pass by. They all knew how out of character this stunt of Katrina's was, and his brother also knew Mason would never physically hurt her.

The next roadblock Mason encountered was the big, beefy bouncer standing at the door, muscular arms folded over his chest, who wouldn't let him walk by.

"Is she leaving with you willingly?" the bouncer asked gruffly.

"No!" Katrina shouted as she tried to kick her legs, which Mason held down with his forearm. "He's kidnapping me!"

"She's such a drama queen." Mason rolled his eyes. "Honestly, no, she's not leaving with me willingly," he said, because, *hello*, he had Katrina flipped over his shoulder and she was yelling obscenities at him. There was nothing *willing* about this particular scenario or her conduct. "But she's had a lot to drink and I'd rather her be my problem than yours."

The bouncer didn't budge, his expression dubious. The dude obviously took his job seriously, and while Mason appreciated him being thorough and cautious, quite frankly, he needed the guy to let them through.

"I can vouch for him." Levi came up to the door, surprising Mason with his support. "He's my brother and I'm a cop," he said, and showed his Chicago PD badge, which he always carried in his wallet.

The bouncer verified the information, and that's all it took to convince him that Katrina was safe with Mason. He finally moved aside to let them past.

"Thanks, man," Mason said to his brother. "I owe you one."

Levi gave him a wry smile. "Yeah, you do."

Behind Mason, Katrina pushed up on her hands so she could look at Levi as they walked through the exit—or glare at him, Mason was guessing.

"You're such a traitor, Levi!" she shouted at him.

Mason heard his brother chuckle before saying, "See you two at some point tomorrow."

As soon as they were finally out on the sidewalk leading to their hotel, Katrina started up again, thrashing and pummeling and cursing. She drew curious stares from strangers, but Mason just smiled and nodded at the passersby as if this was normal for the two of them, and kept strolling toward the Bellagio.

"I can walk, you jerk! Put me down already," she demanded as she smacked and pinched his butt, then growled in frustration when she encountered mostly firm muscle.

"Nope. And quit wiggling around." When she didn't obey, he returned the favor, slapping her bottom so hard she gasped and arched her back from the direct contact. His palm stung from the sharp swat, which meant she'd likely have his handprint on her ass—and Jesus Christ, the image of that possessive mark on her pale skin made his cock hard as stone.

She finally settled down. "I hate you," she said, a pout in her voice.

There was no vehemence behind her words, but Mason knew that for the moment, for whatever reason, she wasn't very fond of him. "I know you do, Kitty-Kat. I just don't know why."

"I already told you," she said, perking up again. "It's because you're an asshole."

He let it go at that, and when they finally reached the Bellagio, Katrina was dead weight over his shoulder and uncharacteristically quiet. He figured she'd either fallen asleep or passed out from the alcohol she'd consumed.

He figured wrong. On the ride up the quiet, vacant elevator, she finally spoke.

"Will you *please* put me down now?" she asked through gritted teeth, her voice clear enough that he knew she'd been awake the entire time. "You've humiliated me enough tonight."

"Me?" he asked incredulously as he bent his knees and anchored her feet on the ground, then helped her to stand. They were facing one another now, and he felt his earlier irritation flare back to life. "I was trying to keep *you* from humiliating yourself up on that bar!"

Her spine stiffened and her gaze shot daggers at him. "I was doing just fine until you came along and ruined my night. I didn't want or need your help."

"Yeah, well, tough shit," he shot back as he jammed his hands on his hips and tried to keep his gaze above her neck when her heaving chest tempted him to look at her perfect breasts pushed up so enticingly by her top. "That's what best friends do, Katrina. They make sure their drunk friends get back to their hotel safely instead of leaving with some random stranger."

Her jaw dropped incredulously. "I can't believe that just came out of your mouth. You're such a fucking hypocrite."

Hypocrite? Was that what she really thought when he was trying to be a good guy and do the right thing? Jesus, he'd never seen her so combative, so angry at him. Sure, they'd had squabbles over their twelve years of friendship, but it was as though her current animosity was an accumulation of weeks, or months, of harboring resentments of some kind.

Before he could demand she explain the hypocrite comment, the elevator arrived on their floor. As soon as the doors slid open, she marched out into the corridor all huffy-puffy and turned toward her suite. He grabbed her upper arm before she could walk too far away, and just like back at the bar, she managed to yank out of his grasp.

She spun around to say something most likely rude and scathing, her hair flying around her shoulders, and he took advantage and did the only thing he could think of to keep ahold of her so she couldn't escape him or the discussion they were going to have. Whether she liked it or not.

Impulsively, his hand shot out and he grabbed the front of her leather pants. He seized the waistband in his fist and jerked her toward him so abruptly that she stumbled on her heels and inhaled a quick breath. Her hands landed on his chest, which allowed her to regain her balance, but she was quick to try and push away from him. She only managed about a foot of space because his grip was strong and unrelenting, and he didn't intend to let her go.

"What the hell, Mase?" she said, her shock as profound as his own.

As he stared into her wide eyes that were a bit too bright with what he would have sworn was *desire*, he wasn't sure if her surprise was a result of him asserting a bit of physical control over her, or the fact that he'd tucked four long fingers between the fly of her pants and her lower stomach. Fuck, his knuckles were grazing the softest, silkiest flesh he'd ever had the pleasure of touching.

He gritted his teeth. Christ, he literally had his hand down her pants.

Asshole that he was, he wanted to push his fingers a little lower, wanted to slide them between her thighs and discover how hot and wet and aroused she was. And deeper, how tight and slick her pussy would feel around his cock as he buried himself to the hilt.

He swore beneath his breath and shook his head, *hard*, doing his best to dislodge the indecent images in his mind, because this was not the time or place. Ignoring the erection thickening against the front of his jeans took equal effort, and he forced his mind back to the issue at hand.

"We're not done with this conversation," he said as he started toward his room while pulling her behind him by the waistband of her pants, being just aggressive enough that she couldn't stop him and was forced to follow. "You've had a bug up your butt the past few months, and you're not leaving my room until you tell me what the fuck is going on and why you're acting so irrationally, and why lately you always seem to be pissed off or annoyed with me."

Reaching his room, he pulled his key card out of his pocket with his free hand and swiped the magnetic strip. The lock disengaged, and he opened the door and hauled her inside the suite. As soon as they cleared the entry area and were in the small living room, he finally released her.

She quickly put distance between them, then whirled around to face him. There was one lamp turned on next to the couch, and the drapes had been pulled open across the floor-to-ceiling windows that overlooked the glittering lights of Vegas at night. The room was slightly shadowed, and while he would have preferred more light, it wasn't a priority at the moment. *She was,* and he refused to be the first one to look away from their current stare-off and give her any kind of advantage.

Her chin lifted a fraction, her expression fierce and angry all over again. With her leather pants, purple-tipped hair, and sleeve of tattoos, she looked like the tough chick she liked the outside world to believe she was. But despite her being a spitfire right now, he reminded himself that beneath that stubborn, defiant exterior, she was the sweetest, most vulnerable girl he knew. She'd survived a hellish childhood, had endured the kind of pain that went soul-deep and would leave most people as twisted and fucked up as he was.

But not his Kitty-Kat. She'd always been his anchor, the one person who kept him balanced and grounded when his life felt as though it was spinning out of control. She'd saved his ass more times than he could count. Maybe it was his turn to return the favor, to try and be patient and understanding—two things that he admitted had never come easily for him.

Except judging by the tight pursing of Katrina's lips and the irritation and restless energy nearly vibrating off of her, she didn't seem to want his empathy. No, she looked like she was ready for an uncivilized altercation with him.

If that's how she wanted to play this out, he'd give her the verbal brawl she was anticipating. He knew how to poke and prod and push her buttons. She wasn't leaving this room until that fucking chip was off her shoulder and they cleared the air between them.

Since she didn't seemed inclined to speak first, he did. "What did you mean when you called me a hypocrite?" he asked, wanting to know what he'd done to deserve that less-than-complimentary label.

"A *fucking* hypocrite," she corrected him. "Because that's what you are. You're so concerned about me leaving with a random stranger—"

"Because you'd been *drinking*," he cut her off, though he knew that excuse was only the partial truth. Watching her dance up on the bar, so lithe and hot and sexy—something she'd never done before—while other men lusted after her, had been the other very strong motivating factor for his rash actions.

"For the record, I am not drunk. Not even close," she said as she folded her arms over her chest— tempting his gaze to stray once again to those plump breasts straining against the front of her corset top.

Damn, he wanted to pluck that tie and set those gorgeous tits free so he could mold them in his hands and take them in his mouth.

"I had two shots over the course of two hours," she went on, oblivious to his wandering thoughts and gaze. "So if I decide to get up on top of a bar and dance and shake my ass, that's my choice, not yours. And if I decide to leave with some hot random guy I want to fuck my brains out—which I was considering since I had so many eager males to choose from," she said in a tone designed to provoke him, "again, I'm a grown woman and that's *my* decision to make."

Oh, yeah, she was all fired up, and he was still trying to get past the disconcerting image of her leaving with a guy she wanted to *fuck her brains out*.

His gut churned with something very green, like envy, and he didn't like it. Not one bit. "I just don't want you to do something you'll regret later." Jesus, when had he become such a goddamn liar? And when had her sex life, and who she chose to sleep with, become his concern?

"Oh, my God," she said incredulously. "Aren't you the one who told me on the plane ride here that I'm too uptight and I don't know how to have a good time? And didn't you bring up the fact that it's been a long while since I've been laid and I ought to take advantage of *Sin City* and find myself a one-night stand and fuck him through the Kama Sutra?" she exaggerated.

He bristled in frustration and irritation, because somehow she'd turned all this around and was now intentionally pushing *his* buttons. "I *never* said that," he replied heatedly as he moved toward her.

"Whatever. Close enough," she said, waving a careless hand in the air. "And I don't know why you're so worried about who I might or might not screw when you were well on your way to hooking up with the first woman you came across in Coyote Ugly!"

As he neared, he saw two distinct emotions pass over her features—hurt, which was quickly followed by . . . *jealousy*? How could that be possible?

Certain he'd misread her fleeting expression, he pinned her with an unyielding look and got a few things off his chest, as well. "I don't know why you've been so irritable lately, or what your problem is, but I'm getting damn tired of trying to figure out your mood swings."

She sucked in an indignant breath. "Want to know what my problem is?" she said on a sudden eruption of outrage. "*You're* my problem, Mason."

She turned to leave, but he was faster. He grabbed her arm, and before she could shake him off this time, he pushed her up against the nearby wall. He flattened his hands on either side of her shoulders to cage her in, and pressed his hips hard against hers to keep her in place until *he* decided they were done talking.

"You don't get to say something like that and just leave without an explanation," he said in a low, harsh voice.

Her glittering green eyes flashed with a quiet but meaningful message for him to *go to hell*. Lips pressed tight together, she gave him the silent treatment—something she *knew* he hated.

He was prepared to wait her out as long as it took. "I have all goddamn night, Katrina."

Seconds ticked into minutes, her willful and obstinate attitude never wavering, nor did her heated gaze. After a while, she tried to move to the side to escape him, but that maneuver only caused their lower bodies to rub together—the soft mound of her sex against the fly of his jeans.

He got hard—so fucking huge there was no way to hide his response to her and the position of their bodies. There was no way she could miss his massive erection, and still, he didn't move, determined to wait her out for the answer she owed him. Except he hadn't anticipated that the awareness and sexual tension between them would grow so increasingly thick he could barely remember *why* he'd trapped her there in the first place. To make some kind of point, yes, but all his aggravation gradually dissolved as male instinct and an undeniable bolt of sexual hunger coursed through him.

Forbidden desire and dark lust swirled through his veins like smoke, testing his control and weakening his will to resist this woman and all the dirty, filthy things he'd fantasized about for too long. Everything below his waistband tightened and pulsed as he stared into her eyes and saw her own carnal cravings reflecting back at him. Flecks of gold glittered in her green eyes, and her full, tempting lips softened and parted, as if inviting him to find out just how sweet she was inside.

He licked his own lips, so starved for the taste of her he felt as though he'd fucking die if he didn't get the chance to experience her flavor. Kissing women, *anywhere*, wasn't something he indulged in often, and he honestly couldn't remember the last time he'd *wanted* to put his mouth on a woman for the sheer pleasure of it.

Sex for him was always quick and uncomplicated, focusing more on his body's needs and chasing that intoxicating high that rushed through him at the peak of orgasm. That physical release allowed him to forget the pain and torment that was always lurking just below the surface, just waiting for a moment of weakness to consume and ravage him.

As a result, his sexual urges were dark and dominant and aggressive. He liked control, and he'd only hooked up with women who wanted the same thing and gave it up willingly, without any expectations. Easy women who made it simple to fuck them and walk away without any emotional involvement.

He'd long ago recognized that out of narcotics, sex, and alcohol, fucking was his self-medicating drug of choice, and his way of coping with the self-destructive urges that threatened to drag him into the depths of a worse kind of hell. But like with any high, the relief was only temporary, and too many times, the aftermath of his actions were rife with regrets and self-loathing. It was a vicious cycle he couldn't seem to escape.

But right now, in this moment with Katrina, he wasn't looking to forget or escape anything. No, he wanted to document every single trembling breath she took, wanted to memorize the flush on her face and the way her pupils dilated with lust the longer they stood in this position, with his cock aching to be inside her. He wanted to remember how small and perfect her soft curves felt pressed against his straining dick, how her increasingly erratic breathing caused her breasts to lift and quiver as the undeniable anticipation between them escalated, second by second. He wanted to bury his face against her neck, inhale her heady female scent, and lose himself in her sweet, luscious body.

Except there would be nothing *sweet* about the way he took her. He didn't know how to do slow or gentle or romantic. When he fucked, he was rough and hard and demanding. Katrina was the one good thing in his life, and he never wanted to taint her with his perverse need to use sex, *to use her,* to ease all those underlying raging emotions from the past that he struggled to keep buried so he didn't hurt anyone or anything.

Especially Katrina.

But as their battle of wills continued, despite the gradual softening changes in her body language, a part of him couldn't deny how much he needed this woman, how badly he ached to be a part of her, in a dozen different ways that were so goddamn wrong he was a prick for even contemplating corrupting her.

But then she made a soft, aroused sound of need in the back of her throat, and his control wavered as an answering fever thrummed through his veins and the beat of his heart echoed louder and louder in his ears. The intensity between them became a tangible thing, until she turned her head away, finally breaking eye contact with him.

And he hated it. Hated that she was trying to shut him out and ignore this fire smoldering between them. He moved one of his hands, his fingers touching the side of her face while his thumb skimmed along her

CARLY PHILLIPS & ERIKA WILDE

lush, damp bottom lip.

"Look at me, Katrina," he demanded softly. This was no longer about their argument or extracting an explanation. No, this was something altogether different, and he was fucking helpless to resist the temptation beckoning to him.

Much to his surprise, she exhaled a shuddering breath that made her breasts tremble and obeyed his command. When her soft green gaze met his once again, he knew he was done for. Gone. Lost. Those beautiful eyes, they saw into the deepest, darkest part of his soul. They always had, and in this moment, he felt so open, exposed, and vulnerable.

She swallowed hard, the hands at her sides coming up to his chest, where she lightly gripped his T-shirt in her fists. Conflicting emotions flashed in her eyes, and he knew she was struggling to deny what they both clearly wanted. What they both *needed*.

"Mason . . ." Her voice sounded strangled and un-certain.

He didn't want to hear any excuses. Didn't want to give either of them a chance to stop what was about to happen. Without thinking of consequences, he pushed her chin up with his thumb and lowered his mouth to hers, finally taking what he'd wanted for the past twelve years.

Chapter Four

THE MOMENT THEIR lips touched, a jolt of blistering heat shot straight to Mason's dick and the word *friends* no longer applied. Because a *friend* wouldn't take possession of this woman's hot, sweet mouth and kiss her hard enough to bruise. A *friend* wouldn't wrap those long, blonde strands of hair around his hand so he controlled the slant of her mouth beneath his and the depth of the kiss. And *Jesus Christ*, a *friend* definitely wouldn't slide a hand down his rigid stomach, curl her fingers around his stiff cock, and squeeze him tight.

Right then, Mason decided that if he was going to hell for touching Katrina, for defiling her, then he was going to take the memory of this one scorching-hot encounter with him, to fantasize about again and again.

Their tongues tangled, deep and wild, and with a

low, primitive growl in the back of his throat, he ground his iron-hard dick against Katrina's palm, dying for the feel of her fingers gripping his bare flesh, stroking him until he came in her hand.

As his appetite for her grew, seducing her mouth wasn't enough. He wanted more. With one last slow, thorough lick inside her mouth and a sexy, seductive bite on her lower lip that made her gasp and writhe against him, he finally ended the kiss and buried his face in the warm curve of her neck.

She smelled like Katrina always did, a light fragrance of cloves and spice that matched her gutsy personality and made him think of sex with her every time he inhaled the arousing scent. He nuzzled her skin and dragged his teeth along her throat, and with a sensual moan, she tipped her head back to give him all the access he wanted.

Bastard that he was, he took advantage of her invitation. He tugged on the ties that held the front of her corset together, pulling on them until they unraveled, loosening her top. With his hands gripping each side, he roughly yanked the bodice down, and since she wasn't wearing a bra, her firm, full breasts were immediately exposed to his avid gaze.

He filled his palms with her plump flesh, kneading her breasts and lightly pinching her tight nipples until she started to pant and squirm restlessly. *So damn hot and responsive.* He devoured her with his eyes, and his mouth watered for a taste. The devil sitting on his shoulder whispered in his ear to *do it.*

He'd already come this far, and while he knew he ought to stop this madness, the moment that Katrina sank her hands into his hair and guided his mouth to her gorgeous tits, there was no way he could refuse. He bent his head and flicked his tongue across her rigid nipple. She jerked shamelessly against him again, the shift of their bodies causing one of his legs to push between her thighs. He nipped at her breast, then sucked her deep into his mouth. Clutching more of his hair until his scalp burned, she brazenly arched her back and rode the thigh wedged up against her sex in an attempt to chase her own orgasm.

Fuck, if she didn't stop her grinding, he was going to come in his goddamn jeans—and that hadn't happened since high school. The friction against his aching cock was so overwhelming, so good, it made him desperate to get inside her. So deep she'd never forget that he'd been there, *that he'd owned her*, if only for those few brief minutes.

He was selfish enough that he'd take whatever he could get.

He released her nipple, and ignoring the sound of protest she made, he removed her fingers from his hair and turned her around so she was facing the wall. He placed her hands flat on the surface and pushed her upper body forward, until her bared breasts were pressed against the cool wall. The position arched her back and made her delectable ass jut out like an offering.

He caressed his palm down her spine and over the

soft, supple leather covering her perfect ass, and considered giving in to the urge to release a bit of his sexual aggression the way he liked best. And if he was honest with himself, he was curious to know what kind of reaction he'd get when he spanked her bottom for the sheer pleasure of it, rather than as a reprimand like earlier.

Before he could change his mind, he brought his palm down and smacked a cheek, firm enough to make his hand smart. She sucked in a gasp and moaned, long and low, the soft sound filled with an unmistakable thrill.

"Mason," she whispered, his name a seductive plea on her lips.

A grin tugged at the corners of his mouth. Her response delighted him and made him hotter than fuck. "Ahh, looks like my sweet Kitty-Kat is a dirty girl who likes to be bad."

She shivered and groaned, and shocked the hell out of him when she admitted in a quiet, submissive whisper, "*Yes.*"

He heard the vulnerable honesty in her voice, and for a moment, he felt as though all the air had left his lungs. It was as though she'd just shared an intimate secret with him, something no other man knew about her, and why did that make him feel so damn possessive? He didn't want to think too hard on that answer, but he did channel that emotion into what he planned to do to her next.

Stepping up behind her, close enough so that his

hard-as-steel cock was pressed against her upturned ass, he settled his hands on her hips. "Spread your legs wider," he ordered, and satisfaction pumped him up when she immediately did as he asked.

He slid his fingers along the waistband of her pants, all the way around to the front, where he unfastened the top button, then slowly lowered the zipper. He tucked the very tips of his fingers into the lace band of her panties, just enough to tease, as well as give her the opportunity to stop what was about to happen.

He could hear her breathing increase, could feel her stomach muscles flutter against his palm in anticipation. He pressed his lips near her ear, his voice gruff as he spoke. "I'm going to slide my hand down to your soft, wet pussy and make you come," he promised, and took her full-body shudder as permission to continue.

When his long fingers dipped between her spread thighs and encountered how *drenched* she was, he had to bite back a ravaged growl. Her sex was so swollen, so slippery and hot, it only took a few strokes across her clit to push her to the edge of orgasm . . . and keep her there. With a cry of need, she moved her hips back and forth against his hand, her sexy little body frantically seeking release.

"Don't stop," she begged without shame, panting hard. "Please don't stop."

"You ready to come for me?" he breathed against her neck, his own cock pushing hard against her ass, aching to be right where his fingers were. *Soon.*

"Yes." Her voice was hoarse, frantic. "*Yes.*"

Another direct, firm caress across that taut bundle of nerves and her entire body began to vibrate, and she exhaled on a low, helpless moan. A rush of moisture coated his fingers as she rolled her hips in tight, tempting circles against his hand and came on a soft, mewling cry of pleasure.

Jesus Christ, he was dying. Dying with the excruciating need to get inside of her. Dying to feel her clench around his cock the next time she came. *He had to have her now*, he thought as he removed his hand from between her legs and quickly tore open the front of his jeans and shoved them down his thighs until his pulsing dick was freed. He withdrew the condom he had in his front pocket—yeah, he never left home without one, manwhore that he was—and with shaking fingers, he managed to roll it down his thick, solid erection.

She'd remained in the same position, her hands braced against the wall, and he pushed her leather pants and panties down, just far enough that he had access to her soft, swollen pussy. He aligned their hips, guiding the sensitive head of his cock between her legs until he reached all that silky moisture and the entrance to her body. She pushed back against him eagerly, so impatient and greedy for him it made his head spin.

As badly as he ached to ram inside of her and rut like a fucking beast, his conscience made him pause.

He had to be sure their lust and desire was one hundred percent mutual. *That she knew what she was doing, and with whom.*

He grabbed a fistful of her hair and tugged her head back so his mouth was right at her ear, trying his best to temper his impulsive need to dominate, even as he knew he'd probably fail because it was who and what he was at the core.

"Tell me you want this," he demanded gruffly. He needed to hear her say the words.

"I want this," she begged enthusiastically as she tipped her hips up, seeking the fullness of his shaft. "Fuck me. *Please.*"

He slid his free hand around to her bare breast and flicked his finger against her taut nipple, making her gasp and her entire body jolt from the sting. Oh, yeah, she liked that. A lot.

"How do you want it, Kitty-Kat?" he rasped.

Her lips parted and her lashes fluttered shut, as if by doing so she'd be able to hide from his penetrating stare. "I need it hard," she murmured. "Rough. Deep."

He smiled against her cheek. *Thank God,* because he wasn't capable of slow and easy on a normal day, and just the feel of the slick folds of her pussy rubbing all over his engorged cock had him on the verge of losing his fucking mind.

He didn't wait another second to satisfy them both. With a merciless upward thrust, he slammed into Katrina, so hard that she lifted up on her toes to accommodate the way he drove his shaft in farther, deeper, until he was buried to the hilt. Their joint moans of pleasure mingled as her tempting body sucked his inside, her tight channel gripping him like a fist as he tried to withdraw a few inches so he could pound into her again and give them both the friction they craved.

"Oh, God," she gasped, whimpering and clawing at the wall as he started thrusting in earnest, pulling out and working himself back in with devastating precision.

She moved in counterpoint to his unrelenting rhythm, grinding her hips back as he surged forward, shamelessly fucking herself on his cock and taking what she needed. It was the hottest, sexiest thing he'd ever seen or been on the receiving end of.

Tightening his hands in her hair, he turned her head and covered her mouth with his, absorbing all those decadent sounds she made as he slid his tongue deep inside, kissing her as thoroughly as he was fucking her. Lust tunneled through his veins, along with a familiar flood of heat that told him he was on the verge of coming. This was usually where his mind shut down, his sole focus zeroing in on getting himself off and reaching for that adrenaline rush that came with his release, and the high that filled him in the aftermath.

But there was no shutting out the overwhelming sensation of being wrapped so intimately around Katrina, of feeling connected to another person in ways that went beyond their physical joining. In ways that felt so damn good and so damn right. *Like she'd been made for him, and no one else.*

He groaned and shuddered as his mouth continued to consume hers, even as his mind railed against the thoughts tumbling through his head. It wasn't supposed to be like this. He wasn't supposed to feel so desperate and wild, and knew this driving hunger was unlike anything he'd ever felt with any other woman before. It was all Katrina. She destroyed his self-control, made him feel so crazed with the primitive urge to mark her and brand her as his so no other man would ever touch her.

Mine. She's all fucking mine.

It was that last possessive thought, as well as Katrina moaning his name against his lips, that sent him right to that sharp edge of a monumental orgasm. Wanting her with him when he climaxed—*something else he normally didn't give a shit about but that mattered with her*—he reached between her legs and rubbed her clit nice and hard. Just how he knew she needed it.

Her body trembled as she came on a soft cry of pleasure, that heavenly pussy milking his dick, clenching and pulsing around him and triggering his own orgasm. The shocking climax ripped through him in the most sublime bliss he'd ever experienced, so intoxicating his vision blurred with the heated ecstasy coursing through every part of his body. Once he was completely spent, he collapsed against her backside with a replete groan. His weight pressed her into the wall as he breathed hard and tried to gain his bearings.

Except as soon as he could think clearly, the first thing that popped into his head was, *what the hell have I done?*

Every last bit of pleasure he'd just luxuriated in evaporated, replaced by a twist of unease coiling in his stomach. Fuck. He needed a moment to get his shit together, to gather his composure so he could deal with what they'd just done, even if the sexual frenzy had been two-sided.

He gently pushed away from Katrina's smaller body, but she didn't move from where he'd pressed her against the wall. Not a good sign at all. *Fuck, fuck, fuck.*

"I'll be right back," he muttered and escaped into the nearest bathroom, suspecting that she needed a moment to herself, as well.

He took care of the condom, fastened his jeans, and washed his hands. He didn't dare look in the mirror, because he wasn't sure he wanted to face the asshole staring back, because despite Katrina's participation, he *knew* he had no business messing around with her. And he'd done it anyway, because he'd been unable to control his goddamn dick and the overwhelming need to finally have what he'd coveted for so many years.

The worst part? In his haste to bury himself in Katrina's pussy, he'd taken her from behind like an animal. He'd missed out on looking into her eyes and watching her expression as she came all over his cock. And Jesus Christ, when had any of those things ever fucking mattered to him? *Never.*

Instead, she could have imagined that it was anyone but him who'd been balls deep inside of her, and might have done just that. The realization chafed him raw, especially when he thought about the words she'd spoken to him in the throes of passion.

I want this, she'd said. Not, *I want you.* She'd wanted the sex, but not *him,* specifically. Her reply was a pretty good indication that he could have been any random stranger he'd told her to hook up with before they'd arrived in Vegas. To get laid because she'd been too uptight.

His hands shook as he dragged all ten fingers through his hair, hating the guilt and self-loathing that twisted in his gut. It was one thing to screw around with women who were in it for the same reasons he was and he didn't have to face on a daily basis, and another thing to take advantage of his best friend and the one person in his life other than his brothers who meant everything to him.

Jesus, he was such a selfish prick and a fuckup. So why would this situation be any different?

Knowing he'd already spent way too much time in the bathroom, he went back out to the small living area in the suite and found Katrina right where he'd left her. She had her leather pants back up and secured, and she'd just finished retying the front of her corset top, her hair a wild tumble around her bare shoulders. She wouldn't look at him, so it was difficult for Mason to get a read on her emotions, but that didn't stop him from appreciating the soft flush on her face that he'd put there, and those damp, swollen lips that he'd kissed and still tasted in his mouth.

The awkward tension between them was nearly palpable. He'd engaged in what felt like a hundred one-night stands, but right now, with Katrina, he was completely out of his element. He struggled to find the words to make it right, if that was even possible.

"Katrina, I—"

She held up a hand and cut him off before he could say anything more and finally met his gaze. "Don't make this into a bigger deal than it was, Mason," she said, her tone even and indecipherable, as was her expression. "It was just sex, and we're both consenting adults and went into it knowing what we were doing."

He'd heard everything she'd said, but his mind was still stuck on the *it was just sex* part of her spiel. Those words felt like a blow—not to his ego or pride, but because she appeared so indifferent when he was still trying to deal with the emotional fallout of what they'd done. *And he fucking didn't do emotional.*

She continued, seemingly oblivious to his turmoil. "The orgasms were great and just what I needed. Maybe now I won't be so uptight," she added with a too-strained smile before she walked the short distance to the door and opened it to leave. "I'll see you tomorrow at the wedding."

Then she was gone, and the quiet in his room was deafening, leaving him reeling with confusion and a big, fat *what the hell?*

In the quiet minutes that passed after her depar-
ture, he came to a startling realization. *This is what it felt
like to be on the* receiving *end of a quick and dirty fuck.*

And he didn't like it. Not one goddamn bit.

❖ ❖ ❖

KATRINA WAITED UNTIL she was locked inside of her
own suite before she sagged back against the nearest
wall and allowed herself to really process what had just
happened with Mason. Amazing, mind-blowing sex,
absolutely. But for her, she knew without a doubt that
that one blistering, unforgettable encounter with
Mason, *her best friend*, had forever altered the way she'd
judge sex with any other man going forward.

It was hard enough that she was in love with Mason and knew he didn't reciprocate those romantic
feelings, but now she had intimate knowledge of what
it was like to experience the kind of exquisite pleasure
she'd always craved. Fears and anxieties had always
gotten in the way of her indulging in a relationship
where she could give up sexual control to a man,
which was why she'd always gravitated toward dating
safe, nice guys who were equally safe, nice, and vanilla
in the bedroom.

Trusting Mason, however, just came naturally because he'd been a part of her life for so long. She knew
he'd never cross the line and physically hurt her. If she
so much as uttered the word *stop*, there was no doubt

CARLY PHILLIPS & ERIKA WILDE

in her mind that he'd do so immediately, which was why she'd asked him—*no, begged him,* she thought as her cheeks heated at the memory—to take her hard and deep and rough. And oh, Lord, had he ever delivered on her request. That one encounter with Mason had been, by far, the hottest and most satisfying sexual experience of her life.

Too bad it wasn't going to happen again. Not only did Mason not do repeats, but she'd seen the panic etching his features after he'd come out of the bathroom, along with the guilt and regret in his gaze. The last thing she'd wanted him to do was apologize, or make excuses for his behavior, so she'd thanked Mason for the orgasms and reassured him that she was fully capable of treating their hookup like the casual encounter it had been.

Yeah, that lie had been excruciatingly painful, but so necessary to protect her heart and emotions. As if such a thing were possible. Her heart was already engaged, now even more so. And her body was forever ruined for any other man.

With a weary sigh, she pushed off the wall and headed toward the suite's master bathroom. She had a long day tomorrow with pre-wedding activities with the girls and the ceremony in the afternoon. She needed a hot shower to help her relax, and then it was time for bed and sleep so she didn't have dark circles under her eyes for the photographs. The last thing she needed was her friends asking her what was wrong. It was bad enough that she'd have to come up with an explanation for what had happened after Mason had hauled her out of the bar, caveman-style, over his shoulder.

After stripping off all her clothes, she stepped into the shower and beneath the spray of water, letting it soak her hair and beat down on her back. Closing her eyes, she brushed her hand along the arm with the butterfly tattoos. Her fingers absently traced the many scars the design concealed, the old wounds a constant reminder of why she gravitated toward more passive men in her dating life. And why she'd been so careful with her sexual partners.

Her childhood had been lousy and filled with emotional upheaval, with parents who had never truly loved each other—or her. Her father had filed for divorce when Katrina was thirteen and moved on with the woman he'd been having an affair with for the past few years, and had never looked back or stayed in touch with Katrina. At such a young age, she'd felt so alone and abandoned, especially when her mother had turned around and married the first man who showed her any interest—an auto mechanic who made Katrina feel uneasy from the day she'd met him. And she'd quickly learned why.

While her mother had worked the evening shift as a clerk at a convenience store, Katrina was left alone with her new stepfather, and it didn't take Owen long to show his true colors. He was intimidating in size, verbally abusive in a crude way, and made inappropriate sexual remarks that made her skin crawl. At thirteen, she'd been an early bloomer, and he'd blatantly leer at her breasts, which were hard to conceal during the summertime in ninety-degree heat and humidity. He'd deliberately brush up against her in ways that would *accidentally* cause him to improperly touch her—his word, not hers—so she'd always lock herself in her room and make herself scarce until her mother got home.

The anxiety of being alone with Owen had escalated to the point that she'd finally told her mother what was happening, confiding in the one person she thought she could trust, who would believe her and make her feel safe. Instead, her mother had been skeptical, and when Carol Sands had *reluctantly* asked Owen about his behavior, the prick had turned everything around and told Carol that it was Katrina who was coming on to *him*. Her mother, who'd always been insecure when it came to men, had opted to believe Owen, and punished Katrina instead.

She'd been devastated, and even now Katrina felt that awful, sickening feeling in her stomach when she remembered the smug look on Owen's face, along with knowing her own mother had sealed Katrina's fate.

One night a few weeks later, Owen had been drinking, and when Katrina had quietly made her way to the kitchen for something to eat, he'd come up behind her and trapped her against the counter. And that's when all her fears had become a horrific reality. In the next instant, he had one hand squeezing hard on her breast and the other shoved between her legs while calling her a whore, slut, and tramp, and informing her *she'd asked for this.*

Katrina shuddered at the terrifying memory as she instinctively crossed her arms over her chest in the shower, letting the stream of water hit her shoulders and cascade down the rest of her body. At almost fourteen, she hadn't been that strong, but with Owen's reflexes not as quick from the alcohol he'd consumed, she'd managed to turn around to face him. When his hands went to the button on her shorts, she'd kneed him in the groin with every bit of strength she possessed, and he'd dropped to his knees in pain.

She hadn't stuck around to see what would happen next. She'd bolted out the front door and run in her bare feet down the street to a park—and had stayed there until morning, when she knew that Owen had gone to work. Her mother hadn't even known that she was gone all night, and even though Katrina had felt violated and traumatized, she'd never said anything to her mother. Why bother when she wouldn't believe her, anyway?

Her self-mutilation had begun after that attack. Angry and hurting deep inside, she'd cut all along her left arm, from her shoulder to her wrist—a series of deep lacerations that had provided her only outlet for the emotional misery. The physical anguish of slicing her skin and watching her wound bleed had been a satisfying distraction to her internal torment. It had been her way to escape reality, and to be in control of *what* kind of pain she felt, when she couldn't control what might happen beyond her locked bedroom door. No, she hadn't understood her actions then, but she did now.

Those were the scars that Mason knew about, the ones created before a gym teacher at school had seen them and gotten her the help she needed to control those destructive urges. The multitude of slice marks along the side of her left hip, however, was a result of a different attack that Mason had no idea had ever happened.

She'd never been able to bring herself to confide in him that one of his friends *had raped her*. Her humiliation and shame had been too overwhelming, and she'd once again resorted to cutting to escape the pain. Luckily, she'd realized her pattern of behavior and sought help once again, but those scars were now a physical and permanent reminder of why she tended to be wary of certain types of men.

She'd been in the shower long enough, lost in her dark thoughts, and the water had turned lukewarm. Not wanting to think about the depressing past any longer, Katrina focused on washing and conditioning her hair, then scrubbing her body clean. Once she was out of the shower and dried off, she slipped on a pair of panties and her favorite well-worn sleep shirt that was soft and comfy. Fatigued after the long day of travel, spa time, and her encounter with Mason, she crawled into bed, determined to get a good night's sleep. She was definitely exhausted enough.

Letting her tired body sink into the mattress, she closed her eyes and turned her mind to tomorrow's wedding, determined to make sure that it was an amazing day for Samantha and Clay. Which meant she needed to act as though everything between her and Mason was normal, that the best sex of her life had never happened, and they were still the best of friends.

And that meant putting on a bright smile, locking away the jumbled mess of emotions churning inside of her, and showing Mason that she was fully capable of moving on after their one-night stand. Just as easily as he could.

Chapter Five

"**H**OW LONG ARE we going to avoid the huge elephant in the room?"

After nearly two hours in Samantha's suite having brunch and now getting their hair and makeup done for the upcoming ceremony, Katrina wasn't at all shocked when Tara finally alluded to last night's confrontation at Coyote Ugly between her and Mason. She *was* surprised, however, that it had taken her direct and outspoken friend this long to say something.

Katrina suspected Tara had held back out of respect for Samantha and making sure the bride-to-be was the center of attention for the first few hours. But now that they were all sitting in a semicircle in the suite's living room, with three hair stylists working on their elegant updos, Tara was obviously ready to push for answers.

"I'm *dying* to know what happened after the two of

you left!" Samantha chimed in, her eyes bright and eager for details. "I can't believe he actually threw you over his shoulder and carried you out of the place like that."

Both women looked amused over Mason's actions, and Katrina tried to keep the story as light as possible without going into those nitty-gritty and dirty details of how that confrontation had ended. "He thought I was drunk and he was trying to save me from myself." She rolled her eyes for emphasis.

Tara snickered, her eyes sparkling with obvious humor. "It didn't appear that way from what Levi and I saw. Mason looked like he was clearly staking a claim on you so none of those other men crowded around the bar had a chance."

"I have to agree," Samantha said as her stylist began pinning all her loose curls into an intricate design at the nape of her neck. "Why do you think Clay tried to step in?"

"Because his brother is a jerk-off?" Katrina suggested sarcastically, causing her own stylist to laugh softly from behind her.

"Mason isn't that bad," Samantha said, defending her soon-to-be brother-in-law, clearly having developed a soft spot for him. "I just think that he's very attracted to you, despite you two being friends, and he's frustrated because he wants something that he knows he shouldn't touch. But he doesn't want anyone else to touch you, either."

Oh, Mason had *touched* her plenty last night, in

ways that made her face warm when she thought about just how skillful those fingers of his were as they'd gripped her hair and slid down between her thighs . . .

"Oh, my God, you're *blushing*," Tara said, calling her out, her tone almost gleeful. "Did you and Mason do the dirty last night?"

Much to her dismay, the flush on her cheeks heated even more. "No!" The last thing she wanted was her tryst with Mason becoming common knowledge when it would *never* happen again. And she definitely didn't want to be known as one of his many conquests, which would put an additional strain on their friendship.

"I think thou protest too much," Tara teased, much too accurately.

"Leave her alone, Tara," Samantha said gently, her gaze so sweet and kind and understanding. "Whatever happened between Katrina and Mason really isn't any of our business unless she wants it to be."

Katrina smiled at Samantha, grateful for her refined upbringing and how aware and considerate she was of Katrina's discomfort. Samantha might not live in her parent's mansion any longer, or even spend much time with them in her old upper-class social circle, but Clay's bride-to-be still maintained those courteous manners that were such an ingrained part of her. Which was what made her so likeable.

"So, how did you and Mason meet?" Samantha asked instead, easily steering the conversation away from last night's activities. "Clay said something about the two of you being friends since your freshman year in high school."

"We did meet our freshman year," Katrina replied, preferring this topic to the other one. "We didn't have any classes together, and I didn't know who he was until he came to my rescue one day when I was walking home from school and three older boys started bullying me."

Samantha's eyes grew round. "What happened?"

Recalling the day, even though it was over twelve years ago, came easily. It had been the second week of school, the temperatures soaring into the high nineties, and she'd worn a zip-up jacket to hide the cuts she'd recently made along her arm. Some had been scarred over, and some had been fresh wounds, but she'd been self-conscious enough that she'd always worn something with long sleeves, despite the weather. She'd lived in an apartment with her mother and Owen in a not-so-great neighborhood, where the kids were ruthless and mean and never missed an opportunity to torment someone they perceived as weaker than them.

That afternoon, she'd been their target, and an easy one at that. She'd been walking home all alone after school and taken a shortcut through the park. But as the three boys approached her, then circled around her and started making cruel comments about how stupid she looked in a jacket considering the heat, Katrina had known the situation wouldn't end well. When she hadn't responded to their nasty taunts, they'd knocked her backpack off her shoulder to the ground, and while one of the boys held her arms back, the other had two unzipped the jacket and pulled it off.

She'd been wearing a tank top beneath, but Katrina shivered as she remembered how exposed and vulnerable she'd felt, and how afraid. Especially when the older boy had started looking at her in that way she'd come to recognize from her stepfather. As the boy had stepped toward her, the sickening feeling swirling in her stomach had escalated, and tears had burned the backs of her eyes. She'd wanted to run, but couldn't since all three of them were surrounding her, leaving her no easy escape.

"Leave her alone," she heard some other male voice shout out.

The leader of the gang glared at someone over Katrina's shoulder. "Who the fuck are you?"

"I'm about to be your worst nightmare," the other kid replied confidently as he finally came into Katrina's view. "Give her back the jacket."

The creep in front of her jutted his chin out belligerently. "Fuck you, man."

Her savior was tall and lanky, and even though he looked younger than the other guys, he was clearly unafraid as he closed the distance between himself and the other boy. Without hesitating, he pummeled the kid in the face, so hard that he stumbled back and landed on his ass.

Instead of coming to their friend's aid, the two other boys immediately backed out of the way, and the one holding her jacket dropped it to the ground as if it had suddenly caught fire.

The guy still on his ass put his hand up to his nose as blood spurted out of his nostrils, his eyes round in shock. "Jesus Christ, I think you broke my nose, you asshole!"

"You're lucky that's all I did," her rescuer said insolently, his body tense and his hands still clenched into fists at his sides as he narrowed his gaze. "Consider this a friendly warning to leave her alone. If any of you so much as look her way again, let alone touch her, I'll break your fucking kneecaps."

One of the other boys put his hands up in a placating gesture, obviously trying to absolve himself of his friend's callous behavior. "We were just playing around, man."

"I don't give a shit what you were doing," he snarled at them, his temper rising again. "Leave. Her. Alone. Now get the fuck out of here before I change my mind and take out my anger issues on all three of you."

With a grumble and choice words muttered under his breath, the kid on the ground got up, and the trio walked away. The guy now standing in front of her wasn't any bigger than those other boys, but he was obviously street tough and didn't take crap from anyone. The fact that he hadn't hesitated to punch the main guy spoke volumes to his aggressive, bad boy, I-don't-give-a-shit personality.

He scooped up her jacket and turned to face her, his features softening a fraction. "Guys who pick on girls are fucking assholes," he said, his concerned gaze meeting hers. "Nobody is ever going to mess with you again; I'll make sure of it. Are you okay?"

She lost her breath along with the ability to speak, and could only respond with a jerky nod. He was gorgeous, with dark, unruly hair and the bluest eyes fringed by the longest black lashes she'd ever seen. And his lips . . . they looked so full and soft, despite that he was a guy. His shirt was old and worn with holes, as were his jeans and shoes, which told her that he came from a family who didn't have much, either.

His fearless actions on her behalf had stunned her, especially since no one had ever defended her before—not even her own mother. His good looks sent her heart aflutter. But it was his vehemence against guys who bullied girls that had her falling madly in love with him right then and there. Until he broke the magical spell by reaching out and skimming a warm, gentle finger over the scabbed cuts all along her arm.

"What the hell happened to your arm?" he asked with a frown.

She instinctively jerked away from his touch. Embarrassment flooded through her that he'd seen the grotesque marks on her skin and now knew just how disfigured and ugly she was. "It's nothing," she said tersely and went to grab her jacket.

He moved it out of her reach, his brows creasing deeply. "It's not nothing. Who did this to you?" he demanded.

She didn't know why, but she was compelled to answer him. "I . . . I did it to myself." And why did he even care?

He didn't push for more answers. Not right then.

Instead, he said very quietly, "I get it," and she knew in that moment that he really did understand her kind of deep, emotional pain, because he'd been there, too. "Maybe someday you'll tell me about it."

After that day in the park, no one had messed with her again. Word had spread around school that Mason

Kincaid would kick anyone's ass who dared to harass her. They'd spent a lot of time together, and he'd become her best friend. Her protector. The one man in her life she trusted without question and who knew things about her that no one else did.

And yes, she'd eventually confided in him about her stepfather, and he'd shared his own horrible family situation. That he had a drug-addict prostitute for a mother who was in prison at that time, and that he'd suffered abuse of his own at the hands of one of his mother's boyfriends. But at least he'd had his brothers, and they all took care of one another. She'd had no one except him.

They'd formed a strong, unbreakable bond, despite Mason's wild and rebellious personality, and despite the fact that she'd spent the past twelve years watching him with other women while loving him from afar . . .

Katrina realized that her mind had wandered—*hopefully not for too long*—and that Samantha was still waiting for her to answer her question about what had happened that day she'd met Mason when he'd confronted her bullies.

"Mason saw that I was all alone and being picked on by three boys," she said, shortening the story. "And when one of the guys wouldn't back away from me, Mason punched him in the nose and knocked the kid on his ass. From that day on, he was like my body-guard, and that pretty much made sure that no one else would ever bother me again."

Samantha gasped in shock, then she started laughing, causing the stylist who was doing her hair to pause for a moment until her giggles subsided. "Oh, my God, so Mason really *was* a ball buster when he was younger! Clay told me he was a handful, and we all know he's still a reckless bad boy. I can only imagine what he was like as a teenager."

"He was a total delinquent," Katrina admitted as her own hairdresser curled a few wisps of hair around her face, then sprayed the pretty style in place. "He drank, smoked pot, ditched school, and pretty much ignored anyone with any kind of authority, including Clay."

"He still does that," Tara said, grinning in amusement. "I mean, who else would get away with banging some chick in the bar bathroom?"

"So true," Katrina admitted, and shook her head as she remembered just how irritated she'd been with Mason for being so crass. "Honestly, Clay tried his best with Mason, but I just think Mason had a lot of anger built up inside of him, and being rebellious to the extreme was his way of acting out."

But even though Mason had repeatedly tested Clay's patience and lived to break rules, she'd always known from the moment she'd met him that day in the park that Mason had a huge heart, even if he didn't believe it himself. She'd seen that caring side the day he'd rescued her from those bullies, and in the way he'd become such a dependable friend to her over the years.

Through the years and during her time in therapy

for her own emotional issues, Katrina had been able to realize that Mason's mother's behavior, and the fact that she'd completely neglected then abandoned all of her kids, had affected him more deeply than he'd ever admit.

Then there was the fact that none of the Kincaid brothers knew who'd fathered each of them, and had never had a paternal figure in their lives that they'd trusted. Katrina knew Mason well enough to know that he felt unworthy of anyone's love, and therefore he did stupid shit to continually test the people around him, to see if he pushed them far enough that they'd eventually leave him, too. It was a reckless pattern that also contributed to his hit-it-and-quit-it attitude with women.

And that was something Katrina didn't think she'd ever be able to change. He wasn't the type to psycho-analyze himself or modify his behavior. The part of him that felt unworthy ruled any impulse or need he might have to change. Not even Katrina's steady presence, unwavering support . . . or love—if Mason would just open his eyes and see it—would change who he was.

"Clay said he even stole a car once," Samantha said, looking completely scandalized by the crime that Mason had committed in his youth.

"Yes, he did," Katrina replied as the girl who'd been doing her hair started applying her foundation. "And he ended up spending some time in juvie for it. But even that didn't straighten his ass out."

CARLY PHILLIPS & ERIKA WILDE

"What finally did?" Tara asked curiously.

"A few months out of juvie when he was seventeen, he got caught spray-painting graffiti on the side wall of this guy's business, which was a tattoo shop." Katrina closed her eyes as the girl applied her eye shadow then liner. "His name was Joe, and instead of filing charges against Mason for vandalism and destruction of property, he made a deal with Clay that Mason would sandblast all the graffiti off the wall and work an entire month in his shop as a cleanup guy, which Mason hated."

Samantha laughed. "I'll just bet he did."

"But Mason has always been artistic, and he loved to draw and was a natural at it." Katrina still had all the drawings that Mason had done for her throughout their years in high school, most of them whimsical and amusing sketches meant to put a smile on her face, and she still cherished each one.

Katrina continued her story as mascara was added to her lashes. "So, during his month of working at the tattoo shop, Joe told Mason that if he proved he could stay out of trouble, he'd teach him a few things about tattooing and let him design for clients. That was the incentive that Mason needed to focus on something worthwhile, and after another six months of being the shop owner's grunt, Mason was offered an apprenticeship. Now, he has his own shop."

"Wow, I had no idea that's how it all happened," Tara said in awe. "Clay must be really proud of Mason."

"He's proud of both boys," Katrina said, having been a part of the Kincaid brothers' lives for so long. "They all had a difficult life growing up, and if it wasn't for Clay being there for Mason and Levi, there's no telling how they all would have ended up. Clay is the one who made sure they stayed together as a family, instead of getting split apart by foster care after their mother ended up in prison."

"And that's why I'm marrying that amazing man," Samantha said with a dreamy sigh. "Because he's got a heart of gold, and there isn't anything he won't do for the people he loves, which makes me one very lucky girl."

A knock sounded on the suite's double doors, and one of the stylists went to let the photographer in, who was ready to take pre-wedding photos of the bridal party.

"Are you ready to get started?" Sara, the photographer, asked Samantha. "We'll begin with the boudoir shots that you requested, then get you in your wedding dress and go from there with your two maids of honor."

Samantha beamed with excitement. "Give me another ten minutes to finish with my makeup, and I'll be good to go."

"Perfect," Sara said with a smile. "I'll get things set up in the bedroom and meet you in there."

Katrina smiled at the blissful look on Samantha's face. Knowing ever having such a fantasy man for herself was highly unlikely, she'd just have to live vicariously through her friend.

But for now, she had to mentally prepare herself for the wedding and to face Mason for the first time since last night and pretend as though everything was back to normal, when that was the furthest thing from the truth.

Chapter Six

MASON COULDN'T STOP staring at Katrina and how stunning she looked as she walked slowly down the aisle of the small chapel in the Bellagio hotel, *and what the hell was that light, pansy-ass fluttering sensation in the pit of his belly?* If that unfamiliar reaction wasn't weird enough, then the increasing beat of his heart as he continued to watch Katrina float toward him like an angel made him wonder if he was getting sick or something. Though he wasn't nauseous and he didn't have a fever.

He exhaled a deep breath that calmed his stomach a bit, but his heart wasn't cooperating. He'd always thought that Katrina was pretty and attractive, but he'd never seen her so breathtakingly beautiful before. Her blonde hair was swept up into some kind of fancy style, and her makeup was soft and subtle, including the pale pink color on those lips he hadn't gotten nearly enough of last night.

The light pink gown she wore was strapless, and the soft, flowing material swirled around her legs with each step she took toward the flower-covered archway. Pearls circled her throat and pierced her ears, and she held a small bouquet of pale pink roses in her hands. She looked graceful and radiant, and all of a sudden, he felt like an infatuated teenager experiencing his first crush.

What the hell was up with that? He'd liked plenty of girls over the years, but he'd never had a *crush* on any of them, which implied emotional and romantic feelings. *And he didn't do emotional and romantic.* Ever.

Standing between Clay and Levi as one of his brother's groomsmen, Mason shifted on his feet and pulled on the collar of his stuffy, buttoned-up shirt. Maybe the tie around his neck was too tight and it was making him fucking delusional. Yeah, he'd grasp on to that excuse, because he refused to allow himself to *go there* with his best friend—even if they'd had the hottest sex ever. And that's all it had been, he firmly reminded himself—one tempestuous, lust-filled encounter that never should have happened between them in the first place.

But it had. And now he couldn't stop thinking about Katrina's uninhibited response to his kiss, his touch, and the brazen way she'd begged for it, hard and deep and rough, just how he liked it . . .

His dick twitched inappropriately in his suit pants, and knowing that Clay wouldn't appreciate him sporting wood during his ceremony, Mason shoved those dirty thoughts out of his head and focused on Tara, who was next to walk down the aisle and took her place next to Katrina, on the opposite side of where the men were standing.

The music changed to a traditional wedding march, and all five of them glanced toward the back of the chapel as Samantha appeared at the double doors in a simple but elegant wedding gown that conformed to her curves and flared out below the knee. She, too, wore her hair up with soft strands framing her face, and Mason could have sworn he heard Clay suck in a quick, sharp breath—and couldn't blame his brother for that uncharacteristic show of emotion. Then again, Clay had become a totally different guy since meeting Samantha—more mellow and patient and unafraid to show a softer side to his feelings when it came to the woman he loved.

Samantha's gaze met Clay's, and she smiled almost shyly as she seemingly glided down the rose-petal-strewn runner toward the bridal party waiting for her. Her eyes sparkled with joy and happiness, and her complexion glowed as she finally came to a stop beneath the arch of flowers and beside the man who was about to become her husband. She handed her bouquet to Katrina, then Clay took both of Samantha's hands in his, and the minister started the ceremony.

Mason glanced past the bride and groom to Katrina, who was watching the pair with a soft expression on her face. It didn't escape his notice that she'd avoided all eye contact with him today so far, and the fact that she was seemingly ignoring him, *as if last night had never happened*, irked the hell out of Mason. Especially when he couldn't stop thinking about the encounter, and her. Not as the best friend she'd been for years, but the sensual woman who'd been his perfect sexual match.

Since Katrina hadn't so much as glanced his way, Mason returned his attention to his brother and Samantha as they spoke their vows and exchanged their wedding bands. Then the minister finally announced that they were now Mr. and Mrs. Clay Kincaid, and Clay could kiss his bride.

His brother did so with a dramatic flourish, bending his new wife over his arm and sealing their vows with a passionate kiss that made the small bridal party laugh and cheer. When he finally let Samantha back up for air, she was grinning from ear to ear and blushing at her husband's very public display of affection— something else that was new for Clay.

The bride and groom headed down the aisle first to exit the chapel, and Mason stepped up and offered Katrina his arm. She looked up at him with a smile, and he couldn't quite gauge whether it was real or forced, then she placed her hand in the crook of his arm to let him escort her out while Levi did the same with Tara. Once they cleared the doorway, Katrina was quick to let him go to congratulate Samantha and Clay once again.

They all toasted with a glass of champagne, then pictures took another hour. Whenever he was required to stand next to Katrina, or touch her, she didn't respond in any way that gave him a solid indication of her mood or feelings toward him. She just acted . . . normal. He should have been grateful that there wasn't any awkward, day-after tension between them, especially since she also worked for him as the manager of Inked, but he found himself growing increasingly annoyed instead, because he so didn't *feel* normal anymore when it came to Katrina and their friendship.

Jesus, he was so goddamn fucked, and he needed to straighten this mess out and get his head back on straight. Hopefully, his dick would follow suit.

"I'm done with the wedding party photos," Sara, the photographer said, much to Mason's relief. "Samantha and Clay, I'd like to get some shots of the two of you by yourself."

The bride and groom went back into the chapel for those couple shots, and Mason decided to confront Katrina head on about last night's hookup—and the fact that it hadn't exactly ended well, though you wouldn't know that by looking at her right now. Maybe if they got everything out in the open and dealt with any lingering issues, *he* could move the fuck on and be satisfied that nothing between them had truly changed. He *needed* that reassurance.

He headed over to where Katrina, Tara, and Levi were standing together, chatting and laughing while they waited for Samantha and Clay to finish up. He came up beside Katrina and lightly touched her arm to get her attention. Startled—since he'd come up from behind her—she glanced at him with wide green eyes, looking very much like a deer he'd just caught in the headlights.

Maybe she's not as immune to me as I thought. "Mind if I talk to you privately for a minute?"

Because he knew Katrina so well, he didn't miss the quick spark of wariness that flashed in her gaze, then she blinked and it was gone. Yeah, she was a pro at hiding her emotions when she wanted to.

"Uhh, sure," she said with a nonchalant shrug.

She followed him down the corridor that eventually led back to the Bellagio Hotel and Casino. When he knew for certain they were out of hearing distance, he stopped and she did the same.

"What's up?" she asked casually, like the good *buddy* she'd always been.

Again, her reverting back to best friends should have relieved him, but he couldn't stop the surge of irritation that was trying to work its way to the surface. He searched her expression for something . . . *more*, but her features were carefully guarded and gave nothing away.

She stared at him expectantly, and he rubbed his hand along the back of his neck, suddenly feeling like a fool. "I just want to be sure. . . Are we okay?"

Her brows rose in surprise at his question. "We're fine. Why?"

She honestly had to ask *why*? As if she didn't remember how goddamn deep he'd been buried in her pussy?

He forced his clenched jaw to relax. "Because after what happened last night, I just want to make sure we're good."

She reached out and patted his chest in a placating manner. "Of course we're good," she said much too easily. "You do this kind of thing all the time, Mason. You and me last night was just like any of your other random hookups."

That was part of his problem, because she hadn't been a casual fuck for him, and he couldn't believe she thought he'd feel like she was just like those random, faceless women. And no, he didn't miss the irony of the situation, which sucked.

"You didn't force me into anything I didn't want to do," she reassured him. "The sex was good, we both got what we wanted, so don't make it weird between us, okay?"

He raised a brow and couldn't stop the words that came tumbling out. "The sex was *just good*?"

She shrugged a bare shoulder. "On a scale of one to ten, I'd say it was a solid seven."

Which was . . . average. He couldn't tell if she was being serious or totally fucking with him, but his damn pride and ego asserted themselves. "You've had better?"

She laughed, clearly enjoying his annoyance. "I don't kiss and compare."

He resisted the urge to *kiss her* right here, in front

of everyone, and make damn sure that there was no *comparison* to how his mouth thoroughly claimed hers. Instead, he shoved his hands into the front pockets of his slacks and changed the subject.

"By the way, you look beautiful in that dress, with your hair up like that."

She smiled softly at the compliment. "You don't look so bad yourself in that nice suit. Hard to believe there's a tattooed bad boy beneath all the finery."

He tugged at the uncomfortable collar and tie. "Trust me, I'd only do this for one of my brothers. I can't wait to get this damn thing off."

Before Katrina could say anything else, Samantha and Clay came back out of the chapel, hand in hand and happy smiles on their faces.

"Who's ready for some dinner?" Samantha asked as they all started toward the hotel and casino area.

"I'd love a burger," Mason said seriously.

Samantha laughed. "We have reservations at Picasso here at Bellagio for an amazing *French* meal."

Mason made a face. He so didn't do fancy-schmancy.

"It's our wedding, Mase," Clay cut in good-naturedly. "So suck it up and mind your manners. It's a fine dining establishment. Don't embarrass us by using your fingers and chewing with your mouth open."

Mason flipped him off, causing his brother to chuckle. "You might be married now, but you're still a dick."

"But now he's *my dick*," Samantha said, then her eyes grew wide in shock. "Oh, my God. I can't believe I just said that out loud."

Levi chuckled. "You've officially been corrupted. Welcome to the family, Samantha."

They arrived at the restaurant and were led out to the private terrace, where a linen-draped table had been set up just for the six of them and they had an unobstructed view of the Bellagio fountains and a water performance every fifteen minutes. Despite Mason's beer budget tastes, they ate the most amazing food, went through a few rounds of drinks, and had their own little celebratory party out on the open patio.

Whenever the fountain shows came on, they took advantage of the music and danced, though it didn't escape Mason's notice that Katrina partnered up with Levi every single time, so he danced with Tara. Despite Katrina's assurance that everything was fine between them, there was no doubt in his mind that she was deliberately keeping her distance. It bugged the shit out of him, but he let her keep up the pretense. For now.

After dinner, they headed to the casinos for some gambling and fun, still dressed in their wedding attire. After a few hours, Clay announced that he had better things to do with his bride than gamble the night away, and they had a marriage to consummate. Samantha blushed, but didn't stop Clay when he swept her into his arms—wedding dress and all—and carried her through the casino to the bank of elevators that led to

CARLY PHILLIPS & ERIKA WILDE

the penthouse suite.

"The night is just getting started," Tara said once Samantha and Clay were gone. "And it's a Saturday night in *Vegas*. What do you say we all go and change out of our wedding clothes and check out the nightclub, Hyde, here at the hotel?"

Levi shrugged, always the easygoing one. "Sounds good to me."

"Sure," Mason said—not ready to call it a night just yet, either. "Count me in, too."

The three of them glanced at Katrina, who gave them an apologetic smile.

"I hate to be a party pooper, but I think I'll pass," she said, *still* not looking at Mason. "It's been a long day and I'm exhausted."

Mason just barely refrained from rolling his eyes at her excuse. And he knew that's exactly what it was— an excuse to avoid spending any more time with him. Fine. She could spend the evening alone in her room, but he was going to Hyde with Levi and Tara, and he was going to have a good time. Hell, maybe what he needed to do was find a willing woman to take his mind off of Katrina and erase last night from his mind so he'd quit obsessing over his best friend.

Yeah, that's *exactly* what he needed to do, he decided.

They all went back up to their rooms to change, except for Katrina, who told them to have fun—and Mason was fucking determined to do just that. Forty minutes later and dressed in a pair of black jeans and a black shirt that left his sleeves of tattoos on display, Mason led the way into Hyde, with Levi and Tara following behind.

The place was starting to fill up, and one glance around at the clientele and Mason knew he'd have no problem finding the distraction he'd come here looking for. The women who'd come to the nightclub for a good time were easy to spot. They wore tight dresses that barely covered their asses, and their tops were so low that their fake boobs were one breath away from popping out.

The interested ones blatantly checked him out, their gazes openly issuing an invitation. They pushed their chests out a bit farther and they smiled flirtatiously. They licked their lips, tossed their hair, and made direct eye contact. Yeah, he knew all the sexual gestures and body language. He'd been around and played the game for so many years that he was a goddamn pro.

Yes, this was exactly what he needed to forget Katrina and last night.

He turned to Levi and Tara, who were looking for a place to sit in the lounge area and have a drink. "Don't wait around for me tonight, kids," Mason said meaningfully. "There's no telling where I'll end up."

Levi raised a brow. "Or with whom?"

Mason shrugged. "You know me so well."

Then he noticed that Tara was frowning at him, her expression etched with unmistakable annoyance. "Why are you looking at me like that?" he asked her.

She pursed her lips. "I just thought that, well, after last night you and Katrina were, well, *you know.*"

He settled his hands on his hips and cocked his head curiously. "*You know?*" he repeated back, not sure what direction this conversation was heading, but he wasn't about to say anything until he knew what *you know* meant.

"Hooking up," Tara clarified.

"Did Katrina tell you that?" he asked, still not giving anything away.

Tara shook her head, still watching him disapprovingly. "No. She said nothing happened, but I would have *sworn* that something had."

So, Katrina had denied having sex with him. She hadn't even confessed the details of last night to her good friend, *because they both knew it wasn't going to happen again.* She obviously wanted to keep it a secret, and out of respect for Katrina, he did the same thing.

"Nothing happened," he said, backing up Katrina's claim.

"Fine," Tara said, and backed down from her protective mode. "Have fun popping your Vegas cherry."

Mason smirked.

"Don't forget that our plane back home leaves tomorrow at noon and the four of us are meeting in the lobby at ten," Levi said, always thinking ahead when Mason preferred to act on impulse, which was why his brother was reminding him of their schedule for the next morning.

"Don't worry, I'll be there," Mason assured him.

"You two don't get into too much trouble tonight," he said dryly, knowing his teetotaler, by-the-book brother wouldn't dare do anything to compromise his straight-laced personality.

As Levi and Tara went into the lounge area, Mason strolled through the nightclub. There wasn't a dedicated dance floor, so everyone was dancing around the booths and tables, and a couple of times, a few women grabbed his arm for him to join them, but he wasn't in the mood to dance.

He flashed them one of his bad boy grins but shook his head and kept on perusing for a woman who stirred his interest, and his cock. Usually, that wasn't a problem for him. But tonight, it seemed that his dick was being particular, and that realization was beginning to irritate the shit out of him.

He glanced over at the bar. A curvy brunette in a short black dress with a halter-style top that plumped up her breasts was sitting on a barstool in the far corner, sipping a cocktail and watching him. As soon as his gaze met hers, she smiled at him, then patted the vacant chair next to hers, beckoning him over.

Figuring he was running out of options because he was being too damn picky, he walked over and slid into the seat. She set her empty glass on the surface of the bar as her bright red lips curved seductively at the corners, her eyes filled with an unmistakable invitation that he knew would lead to exactly what he was here for.

"Care to buy me another drink?" she asked in a

sultry voice as she slowly, suggestively, slid her finger around the rim of her glass.

A drink and polite formalities first. "Sure," he said amicably. "What are you having?"

"An apple martini."

Mason motioned the bartender over and placed their order. "She'll have an apple martini, and I'll have a Bulleit neat."

The bartender moved away to make their drinks, and the woman turned her body toward him on her seat and pushed out those breasts toward him. Yeah, he had no doubt she'd done this before, too. Perfect.

"So, are you visiting Vegas, or do you live here?" she asked as she crossed one slender leg over the other.

"Visiting from Chicago," he replied, wishing like hell his body would get on board with his plan to get laid, so he could get it over with. "I'm here for my brother's wedding this weekend."

"That's nice. Are you with anyone here at the club?"

He didn't think she cared about his brother and Tara, but was instead asking about a significant other. Katrina once again popped into his mind, and the unexpected guilt that twisted in his gut made him shift in his seat. He had nothing to feel remorseful about, he told himself, and tried to focus on the woman next to him.

"No," he replied. "I'm here on my own."

"Me, too," she said, and licked her bottom lip.

All Mason could think about were *Katrina's* lips, and all the dirty, filthy things he still wanted to do to that soft, warm mouth. He hadn't gotten nearly enough last night.

The bartender delivered the drinks, and Mason pulled two twenties from his wallet and gave them to the guy. "Keep the change."

"Thanks, man," the server said, and moved on to another customer.

The woman took a generous sip of her martini and placed her hand on his thigh, clearly making the first move. Normally, his cock would perk right up and he'd be raring to go. He didn't feel so much as a twinge of sexual desire. Nada. Nothing. His dick was giving him a big ol' *fuck you*. How in the hell was he going to shake off Katrina if his body refused to cooperate?

"So, you're here all alone, and so am I," the woman said as she brazenly skimmed her fingers up his thigh until her hand was palming the front of his jeans. "How about we finish these drinks and go somewhere more . . . private?"

She was massaging the bulge beneath the zipper with expert hands, and he waited for it to happen, for his shaft to get hard and . . . zilch. Beyond frustrated, he closed his eyes and instantly recalled the way Katrina had cupped him through his jeans last night, how she'd rubbed and squeezed him until he'd thought he was going to come in his pants.

His cock suddenly throbbed at the erotic memory

and *finally* started to stiffen, but now *this* woman's caresses felt dirty and wrong.

"Fuck," he swore irritably, and pushed the woman's hand away, harder than he'd intended.

She sat back, looking more pissed than hurt. "Jesus, are you gay?"

He would have laughed if he weren't so damn aggravated at the entire situation. "No, I'm not fucking gay."

"You don't have to get defensive about it," she said peevishly. "They have things you can take for that sort of . . . problem."

This time, he did laugh, the sound low and harsh. The only thing that would cure him of his problem was Katrina herself. Until then, his own dick was cockblocking him. Fucking fantastic.

He tossed back his whiskey and gave the woman an apologetic glance. It wasn't her fault that his cock had suddenly gone on strike. "I'm sorry," he said, and decided to go before he embarrassed himself further.

He didn't bother to tell Tara and Levi that he was leaving, and they'd probably assume that he was off somewhere getting laid, which would have been the case if his penis weren't on protest. Feeling uneasy and restless, he went back to the casino and sat down at one of the high-dollar blackjack tables that required a minimum of one hundred dollars per bet.

After losing five hundred dollars in the span of five minutes, he did the smart thing and stopped . . . but there was no shutting down his undeniable need for one woman, and one woman only. *Katrina*. And that realization scared the shit out of him, because it made him feel way too vulnerable, like he was losing control not only physically but emotionally, too.

He craved the relief that only she could provide, and he needed it badly. One time and she'd become his fix, and he desperately needed one more hit so he could fuck her out of his system, so that when they returned to Chicago, they could revert to being best friends, because that's all he could ever be for her. He was too fucked up, and she deserved a man who could love her wholly and completely.

One more night. That's all he needed, he told himself like the addict he was as he headed toward the hotel elevators, that frantic anticipation already surging through his veins. Lust. Desire. That was what he knew. What he understood. And once he had a few hours to wring every ounce of pleasure from Katrina's body, he'd be able to walk away, leaving them both satisfied, and still friends.

Chapter Seven

Katrina was curled up on one of the soft, comfortable armchairs in the suite's living room reading a book in an attempt to distract her thoughts from what, or rather *who*, Mason was doing, when someone knocked on her door.

She frowned. She wasn't expecting room service, but when the rapping sound came again, this time more firmly, she set her e-reader on the coffee table and padded in her bare feet to the entryway. She glanced through the peephole and sucked in a shocked breath when she saw Mason standing on the other side.

She couldn't imagine what he was doing here when she'd fully expected him to be off cavorting with another woman by now. Having spent the past hour tormenting herself with all sorts of sordid scenarios, she was both relieved and curious to know what he wanted this late at night. And just in case it was important, or an emergency, she opened the door, regardless of the fact that she was wearing a tank top without a bra and a pair of drawstring pajama shorts.

She noticed right away that he looked tense—both his body and his expression. His hair was a mess, too, as if he'd repeatedly combed his fingers through the strands, and a frustrated frown pulled at his brows.

"Is everything okay?" she asked anxiously.

"Everything and everyone is fine," he rushed to reassure her, as if knowing that she'd automatically think the worst. He exhaled a deep breath, which seemed to ease some of his tension. "Can I come in?"

She nodded. "Yeah, sure."

Stepping aside, she let him walk past, but deliberately didn't lead him into the living room. They remained in the entryway, because whatever his reason for being here, if there wasn't an emergency, she decided he wouldn't be there for long. Then it dawned on her that he was probably there to rehash the conversation they'd had after the wedding and ask her *again* if she was okay. Ugh. She so didn't want to go *there* again.

"Mason . . . I'm really not in the mood to talk," she said with a sigh.

The light in his eyes changed, and his expression turned almost wolfish—a look she recognized from when he zeroed in on a woman he wanted, but that he was now directing at *her*. Everything inside of Katrina automatically responded to that suddenly predatory gaze. Her heart raced and her body tingled in awareness.

He glanced down at where her tank top molded to her breasts, her nipples now poking hard against the fabric. A sinful smile tugged at the corner of his mouth when he met her gaze again. "That's good, because I'm not here to talk."

He took two slow steps toward her, and she instinctively backed up the same amount—and gasped when her ass encountered the wall behind her. Without hesitating, he flattened his palms on either side of her head—just as he'd done last night, right before everything had turned hot and wild between them.

She tried, desperately, not to give in to him like his normal easy conquests. "Then what are you here for?"

He shifted in front of her, deliberately brushing his body against hers, just lightly enough to tease. "I'm here to see if you're in the mood for a few more orgasms," he said huskily.

She blinked at him, then laughed softly—which helped to alleviate any last lingering strain between them. And it definitely piqued her interest. "You're such a sweet-talker, Mase."

He shrugged. "No sense beating around the bush when it's something I know we both enjoyed last night."

She couldn't deny that, and then she had a thought. "Oh, my God, did you strike out at Hyde?" she asked incredulously.

Something flickered in his gaze, a brief flash of annoyance that he covered just as quickly. "I had offers, but none that appealed to me."

"And I do?" The thought sent a thrill through her, and caused her entire body to feel warm and liquid.

"Let me test that theory," he said, his voice underscored with humor as he grabbed her hand and placed it at the crotch of his jeans. With his gaze searing into hers, he curled her fingers around the thick outline of his shaft and shuddered.

"Fuck, *yeah*, you appeal to me," he said, a combination of relief and triumph chasing across his gorgeous features as his cock seemingly pulsed against her palm. "And I'm betting if I pushed my fingers between your legs, you'd be wet and slick with an equal amount of desire."

There was absolutely no way she could deny that claim, so she didn't even try. "You're so damned cocky."

"I am," he agreed shamelessly as his eyes turned a dark, hot blue and he rubbed her hand harder against his solid erection that had grown to twice its size since she'd first touched him. "Which means you get all the *cock* you can handle."

She swallowed hard, her mind spinning. She'd be lying to herself if she said she didn't want one more night with him. But she also knew that's all this could be, because she wasn't the kind of woman who could be his fuck buddy on a regular basis and not let her emotions get in the way. Her feelings for him were already so complicated, and things were going to change between them once they returned to Chicago. They had to, for her own heart and sanity.

But tonight . . . she wanted Mason and all that aggressive dominance that excited her so much. And it was imperative that he understood that tonight would be on her terms.

"I have one condition," she said, trying her best to think straight when he settled his big, warm hands on her hips and slowly slid them upward, pushing the hem of her tank top up as he went.

"And what's that?" he asked huskily, his palms stopping at the indentation of her waist.

She nearly moaned as his thumbs lazily grazed her stomach, making her nipples pebble so tight they ached. "What happens in Vegas stays in Vegas," she finally managed to say. "Once we get back to Chicago, no more hooking up. This is it."

"Agreed," he said with a nod, then grinned. "It'll be our dirty little secret."

"I'm totally on board with dirty." And she was dying for him to close the distance to her breasts and take them in his hands.

"That makes two of us." He continued stroking his thumbs around her navel and tipped his head to the side. "You said today that the sex last night was just good."

"Yes," she replied, though it wasn't true. At the time, she'd meant to irritate him and, yes, even deflate his ego a bit, which had worked. Now, she realized it would give him something to aspire to. "It was a solid seven."

He smirked. "Tonight, we're not stopping until you scream *ten*," he promised, and moved back just a few inches so he could unbutton his black shirt. "Is that understood?"

She shivered at the darker, more assertive tone of his voice. "Are you sure you're up for that kind of challenge?"

"Abso-fucking-lutely," he said on a low, fierce growl. "You up for more filthy, hot, rough sex?"

She bit her bottom lip as she watched the front of his shirt gradually open, revealing the broad expanse of his chest and the beginning of his ripped and toned abdomen. Oh, yes, filthy, hot, rough sex with him sounded so decadent. "Yes, please," she said much too eagerly.

He chuckled as he shrugged out of his shirt and tossed it aside. "Then let the games, and the orgasms, begin."

Framing her face in his hands, he tipped her head up to his and covered her mouth with his own. Her lips automatically parted beneath the pressure of his, and his tongue swept inside for a devouring kiss. She moaned as he licked at her mouth, as his teeth bit her bottom lip, then he came back for a hotter, deeper invasion. As if he couldn't get enough of her. As if he'd die if he didn't keep kissing her.

Needing to touch him, she placed her hands on his hard chest and dragged them downward, using her thumbs to trace the tight, corrugated muscles of his stomach until she reached his jeans. She followed the waistband around to his bare back and skimmed her flattened palms up his spine. She'd seen him with his shirt off plenty of times, but feeling his warm, smooth flesh beneath her hands was a luxury and a treat.

Groaning against her lips, he ground his hips against hers. The metal buckle of his leather belt dug into her belly, and his denim-clad cock nudged her mound. Her sex wept with need, and she had to resist the urge to climb him like a tree and wrap her legs around his waist so that heavy bulge in his pants could give her the relief her body was clamoring for.

Instead, she sank her fingers into the muscles along his shoulders, then raked her nails all the way down his back again. He shuddered and wrenched his mouth from hers, breathing hard.

"*Fuck*," he rasped harshly, even as his lips curved with seductive amusement. "My Kitty-Kat has claws and isn't afraid to use them."

His hands still clasped her jaw, and he swiped one of his thumbs across her swollen and damp bottom lip, then pushed it past her teeth. Holding his gaze, she closed her mouth around his finger and swirled her tongue around the digit, knowing full well where his imagination would go.

His eyes darkened with lust. "God, your mouth . . . I want to feel it wrapped around my cock just like this, and watch as you swallow me deep."

He slid his finger back out with a suctioning *pop* of sound, and because she wasn't about to give it up so easily, she taunted him instead. "Make me."

A hot, depraved look passed over his features, letting her know that he had absolutely no qualms about accepting her dare. He slid one of his hands through her hair, pulling it away from her face until he had a fistful gathered at the back of her head. He tightened his hold on the strands with a twist of his fingers, making her very aware of who was really in charge tonight. *He was.*

Her heart raced, and there was nothing she could do to stop the rush of moisture that dampened her panties.

"Get on your knees," he ordered, and with the wall at her back and his hands gripping her hair and pulling her *down*, she had no choice but to obey.

She knelt in front of him and awaited his next command.

"Good girl," he murmured, though his hold on her hair didn't loosen at all. "Now open my jeans and take out my cock, but be very careful because there is *nothing* separating my dick from that zipper."

So, he'd gone commando. Her breathing escalated in anticipation as she unbuckled his belt and unfastened the top button. Oh-so-cautiously, she dragged the zipper over the massive erection straining against the front of his pants and freed his shaft. Last night, she hadn't had the pleasure of seeing him naked like this, had only felt the size of him inside her, and dear Lord, even his cock was gorgeous. Thick and smooth and perfectly shaped, and just as big as she'd imagined.

CARLY PHILLIPS & ERIKA WILDE

With his free hand, he fisted his fingers around his erection and pumped the length once, twice—slowly, expertly, until a bead of pre-cum seeped from the slit. Without thinking, she licked her lips. The erotic sight of him stroking his own shaft, and his proof of arousal, made Katrina's thighs clench together in an attempt to ease the growing ache in between. It didn't work. No, it only made her more desperate. Needier.

"Take me in your mouth, Kitty-Kat. *All of me.*" He pressed the head against her bottom lip, and she licked away the drop of fluid on the tip, making him groan raggedly. "Fuck, I need to feel your soft tongue sliding all the way down my cock. Do it. *Now.*"

Placing her hands on his hard thighs, she opened wide as he pushed his way inside. She took him all the way to the back of her throat, then let him slide back out until she was just sucking on the crown. She did it again, slow and slick, and he cursed beneath his breath and braced a hand on the wall behind her for better leverage. With his other hand wrapped up in her hair, he guided her head, and she let him dictate the pace, the rhythm, giving him all the control, all the power.

With every deep stroke, his salty taste filled her mouth and his male scent filled her senses. She sucked him in, then back out, again and again, even as his thrusts grew harder, more frantic. She reached between his legs and palmed his balls, and when his groans increased in volume and he shouted out a series of "*yes, fuck yes, fuck yes,*" she continued to massage them until they tightened and his body began to shake

106

and she knew she'd driven him to the edge. She relished the fact that she'd brought him to this delirious point, and realized that for the first time ever, she wasn't going to pull away from the orgasm about to erupt.

No, she wanted all of Mason.

"Jesus . . ." he rasped. His legs started to tremble as she pulled him to the back of her throat once more and swallowed around him. "Need you so fucking bad . . . Your mouth is so hot, so greedy . . . I'm going to come so fucking hard . . ."

He drew quick, shallow breaths, and then his shaft pulsed against her tongue, his hips jerking erratically as he climaxed with a raw shout of pleasure that gave her an equal amount of satisfaction. When he was completely spent, he dropped his head against the wall and released her hair, allowing her to finally move.

She glanced up, her gaze taking in all those amazing muscles along his abdomen. Combined with those artistic sleeves of tattoos, his body was a work of art. Unable to resist, and since he was still in the process of recovering, she pressed an open-mouthed kiss right below his navel and smiled when he groaned.

With her tongue, she licked her way upward, leisurely following the pathway of all those delicious ridges and grooves along his stomach. When she scraped her teeth across a nipple, he hissed out a startled breath and cupped a hand around the back of her neck to haul her all the way up so she was standing in front of him again.

Without hesitating, he kissed her again, thoroughly, deeply. When he had his fill, he pulled back and touched his forehead to hers. "That mouth of yours is fucking lethal."

Her body buzzed from his compliment, and she grinned. "And I think your *average* just got elevated to an eight."

He lifted his head and stared into her eyes, an arrogant smile curving his lips. "Then it's a good thing I'm not done with you yet, so there's still room for improvement."

She laughed. "You can certainly try."

"Oh, I intend to." He zipped up his jeans but left the belt hanging open, then moved out of her way. "Go sit on the couch and we'll get started."

Her anticipation was off the charts, and her legs shook as she followed his order and sat down on the nearby couch, still fully clothed. She watched him approach, her excitement increasing with every step he took toward her. When he was finally in front of her, he went down on his knees, reached up to untie the drawstring of her pajama shorts, then dragged them and her panties down her legs and off at the same time.

Her breath hitched in her lungs, and she kept her knees pressed together as she started to remove her tank top, too.

He quickly stopped her. "Leave it on. I want to savor one thing at a time," he said huskily, but didn't touch her like she wanted him to. "And right now, it's all about getting my fill of that sweet spot between your thighs. Spread your legs nice and wide for me, Kitty-Kat, so I can make you purr."

Realizing just how exposed she'd be, that she'd never been so brazen with another man before, she hesitated.

"Come on, sweetheart," he cajoled softly, as if sensing her sudden bout of nerves. "Show me that gorgeous pussy. I promise I'll make it worth your while."

He wasn't demanding, but she couldn't deny the need she heard in his low, mesmerizing voice. She parted her legs about a foot, not nearly enough for him to appreciate the view he wanted—and maybe this time she was deliberately teasing him, just to see how far she could push Mason before he reverted to that hot alpha male who took control.

It didn't take long.

"*More*, Katrina." This time, he sounded impatient and much more assertive, and she gasped as he placed his palms on her knees and forced them as wide as they would go, shredding every last one of her inhibitions.

Her fingers sank into the couch cushions as he stared at the swollen folds that had parted like a flower for him, pouty lips that glistened with so much dewy moisture. She watched as his big hands slowly slid up the insides of her thighs, and she made a soft, mewling sound in the back of her throat when he reached her sex and brushed the pads of his thumbs along the outer crease, making her desperate to feel his caresses on all that sensitive, throbbing flesh.

"Mason," she begged frantically. "Please touch me. I need to come so badly."

Satisfaction gleamed in his blue eyes. "How do you want my mouth and tongue on this pussy, baby?" he asked as he placed a hot, wet kiss on the inside of her thigh and slowly licked his way up to the apex, stopping just short of her core. "Soft and slow, or hard and fast?"

"Both," she said, unable to choose when her mind was already starting to short-circuit. "I want both."

"Greedy girl," he murmured, his breath scalding her seconds before he buried his mouth between her legs and completely obliterated her senses.

He started soft and slow, his tongue lapping the entire length of her sex and curling around her clit with teasing swirls, causing her entire body to arch toward that wicked mouth in a silent plea for harder, deeper friction—even though there was nothing she could do to force him to rush.

With every deliberate lick, every persistent stroke, every dip of his tongue pushing inside of her, he gave her no choice but to take the pleasure he inflicted, at his own sweet pace. It was maddening, breathtaking, and when he slid two fingers deep and rubbed along her inner walls, the overload of sensation had her delirious for release.

Whimpering with need, she shoved her fingers through his hair, shamelessly pulling him closer, and he finally obliged, latching on to that sensitive bundle of nerves and using his teeth and tongue to propel her toward an unbelievable peak. Her entire body jolted with the force of the orgasm surging through her. Her head fell back against the couch and she closed her eyes, crying out his name as a tidal wave of ecstasy crashed over her, leaving her wrecked and over-whelmed from so much sensation.

She felt him move away, and she didn't know how much time had passed before she was able to lift her head and open her eyes again. He was sitting, com-pletely naked, in the single armchair across from where she was sprawled on the sofa. He'd obviously had enough time to take off all his clothes, and he was clearly way more comfortable in his nudity than she was in hers as he reclined casually, his long, solid legs slightly spread.

He was so gorgeous and hot and magnificently male. His shaft was thick and hard again, curving up against his lower abdomen, and she was shocked to feel a renewed thrum of desire pulse through her at the realization that he wasn't done with her just yet. At least she hoped he wasn't.

He tipped his head to the side and gave her a smug smile. "Well?"

She knew what he was waiting for, but she wasn't about to feed his ego too quickly. "Nine," she said, and watched as he arched a dark brow at her. "That was definitely a nine."

He lifted the belt she just realized he'd been hold-

CARLY PHILLIPS & ERIKA WILDE

ing in his hand and snapped the leather strap, causing her heart to double its beat and a secret thrill to zing through her—proof of just how much she did trust him, especially since she had no idea what he intended to do with that belt. Whatever it was, she knew it would lead to pleasure, not the kind of pain that left scars on her soul or even her body, and that knowledge soothed any unease she might have had.

"A *nine*," he drawled, his voice infused with sarcasm. "All right then, let me try *harder* this time. Get on your hands and knees and crawl over here to me, like the obedient Kitty-Kat I know you can be," he dared her.

Going down on all fours, she did as he ordered and moved toward him slowly, seductively, her hands and knees moving in sync. She put an extra sway into her hips, and reveled in her own bit of satisfaction when her sensual ploy didn't go unnoticed by him. By the time she reached Mason and knelt in front of his chair, the heat and hunger burning in his gaze were hot enough to sear her.

"Come up here and straddle my thighs," he said, his voice sandpaper rough.

She moved up onto the chair, spreading her knees wide apart on either side of his thighs so she was sitting astride his lap. A very small bit of space separated her aching sex from his engorged shaft, but knowing it was oh-so-close made her all the more anxious to feel his cock deep inside her again. He didn't touch her, and it was pure agony waiting for that initial contact, and where it would be.

"*Now* you can take off your top so I can see your pretty breasts," he said as a slow, wicked grin claimed his lips. "And if you're good, I might even touch them and suck them."

Oh, yes, please. Without hesitation, she pulled her tank top over her head and dropped it on the floor beside the chair. Completely naked now, she felt her heart beat wildly in her chest. His gaze took in her breasts almost reverently, and beneath his avid stare, her nipples puckered into tight, hard points, begging for his warm, wet mouth. She was already so aroused she had to swallow back a needy moan.

He lifted the belt and slid the leather across his palm, reminding her of its existence. "Put your hands together behind your back."

And *now* she knew what he had in mind. Realizing just how vulnerable and defenseless that would make her, she had a moment of uncertainty as her thoughts tumbled back to the past and that awful night when she'd been so powerless against another man's calculating intentions.

She must have hesitated too long, because a small, concerned frown marred Mason's brow. "Do you trust me to make you feel good, Kitty-Kat?" he asked softly.

She swallowed hard. Mason was nothing like Connor and would never manipulate or hurt her—and she hated that another man had instilled that deep-seated fear inside her. She also knew Mason would respect her decision if she didn't give in to his request, but she wanted so badly to overcome that unpleasant memory, and what better way to do that than to replace it with the kind of pleasure she knew Mason could give her?

She exhaled a deep breath and, along with it, her uncertainties. "Yes, I trust you," she said, and put her hands together at the base of her spine as proof.

He searched her expression, and she loved that he cared enough to be concerned about her physical and emotional well-being. He must have seen the assurance he was looking for, because he finally reached behind her with the belt. As he held her gaze, he looped the leather strap around her wrists and through the buckle, securing it tight enough to restrain her but loose enough that it wasn't uncomfortable.

The position pulled her shoulders back, which in turn thrust her breasts out like an offering. He took them in his hands, squeezing her flesh and rolling her nipples between his skillful fingers until that tugging and pinching became almost too much to bear. She moaned, her sex clenching as he rubbed his thumbs in slow, torturous circles around her areolas.

"Jesus, you are so goddamn beautiful and perfect," he said, his tone shockingly possessive as his gaze followed his hands as they skimmed along her waist, then disappeared around to her backside. "Every single fucking inch of you."

She treasured those sweet uncensored words, because it wasn't often that she thought of herself that way when she was so emotionally and physically flawed. But right now, with Mason, she felt imperfectly perfect, and yes, beautiful, too.

His hands splayed over her bottom, gripping her ass as he hauled her forward, until the lips of her sex were pressed against the length of his shaft in a hot, wet, intimate kiss. "Feel that, baby?" he asked as he rolled his hips, grinding his cock against her drenched folds and coating himself with all the slick moisture from the last orgasm he'd given her. "I already came once in your mouth, and I'm already so fucking hard for you again."

She bit her bottom lip as he continued to rock against her core, the pressure and friction making her body come alive all over again. With each intentional stroke, the ache between her thighs became an unrelenting throb, and she gyrated her hips against his erection, giving him a dirty, filthy lap dance that had him clenching his jaw and his chest rising and falling with harsh breaths.

A dark, dominating growl rumbled in his chest, and his fingers dug harder, deeper, into the soft flesh of her ass. "That's it, Kitty-Kat. Rub your soaked pussy all over my dick. Make yourself come on my cock."

His wicked words and the command in his voice were like a direct link to her clit, making those sensitive nerve endings scream with need. She wanted to grab ahold of his shoulders so she'd have some kind of anchor when she flew apart, but since that wasn't possible, she dug her nails into her palms as she continued to rub herself all over him. The lust swirling inside of her magnified, and when she met Mason's glittering blue eyes as he watched her with such heat and desire, there was no holding back the orgasm that crashed over and through her, or the shuddering moans that escaped her lips.

Before she had a chance to fully recover, he'd rolled on a condom, and then his hands were gripping her waist and lifting her up on her knees so that he could position the head of his cock at her opening. Then he pulled her down on his shaft, plunging so hard and deep she cried out at the initial shock of it.

She was impaled to the hilt, and he didn't move. When she opened her eyes and looked into his, she realized he was giving her a moment to adjust before he let loose, and there was no doubt in her mind that she was in for a rough ride. She could feel the tension in his body from holding back and the pulse of his cock inside her, could see the muscle in his cheek tick as he slowly slid his hands down to her hips.

Unexpectedly, his expression changed to confusion, and he frowned as his fingers feathered back and forth over her left hip. It took her a moment to realize what he'd discovered, that he could feel the multitude of thick, ugly, jagged scars that were embedded there. She'd kept them hidden from him for so many years, along with the painful and humiliating secret that had come with those permanent marks on her skin.

He only knew about the scars on her arm that were now covered with the butterfly tattoos, and believed she'd never cut again after she'd gotten that initial help after her stepfather's abuse. She saw the questions in his gaze, and she tried not to panic.

"Katrina?" His voice was so gentle compared to the physical war she knew he had to be battling with his very aroused body.

She shook her head frantically. "Not tonight, Mase," she said, making it clear that particular topic was off-limits. "I just need you to fuck me and make me feel good, and give me that ten you promised."

That prompted a smile out of him, which she'd been hoping for, and he nodded in understanding. "That I can do. But this conversation isn't finished," he said.

She had no doubt he wouldn't let the subject go. But for now, she wanted to forget, so she rocked her body into him, redirecting his thoughts back to the pleasure they both craved.

MASON LAY NEXT to Katrina in the king-sized bed in her suite, her soft, warm body tucked in front of his, and his arm around her waist as she slept. Having been best friends for twelve years, it wasn't the first time they'd cuddled, but it was certainly the first time they'd done so completely naked.

That made him grin. It was after two in the morning, and he knew he needed to go, but he couldn't bring himself to separate from Katrina just yet, because once he walked out that hotel door, *this* would be over. He'd never experienced closeness on this level before. This connection to a woman that was more than just a physical high and release needing to be satisfied. More than an addiction and adrenaline rush he'd spent so many years chasing in order to keep painful memories of the past at bay.

For all his random sexual encounters, Mason had never, ever felt so sated, and knew it had nothing to do with the half-dozen different ways he'd fucked Katrina. This feeling was . . . different. He felt calm *inside*, content in a way that was foreign to him. They'd thrown some very hot sex into the mix of their friendship, and if he were a better man instead of a selfish asshole, he never would have allowed them to cross that line. But they had, and right now, in this quiet moment when Katrina was all his, he had absolutely no regrets. . . and hoped she didn't, either.

But that didn't change the fact that they both had agreed to leave this fling behind in Vegas, which he knew was for the best. Phenomenal, mind-blowing sex was one thing. Giving Katrina what she needed emotionally was something he just wasn't equipped for. He didn't do relationships for a reason. Hell, he was damn lucky that they'd remained friends for the past twelve years, that she'd put up with his shit for that long, and he'd be a fool to screw that up for the sake of being fuck buddies. There was no way they could continue to have sex and at some point not have it interfere with or complicate their friendship, not to mention conflict with her working for him at Inked. It wasn't a risk he was willing to take.

Bottom line, Katrina was too important to him, and the thought of her not being a part of his life on a regular basis made his stomach twist with dread. She was his *person*, the one who kept him centered and accepted him, despite all his stupidity, his less-than-stellar choices, and all his emotional hang-ups, and he'd be lost without her in his life.

But he had to admit, the fact that she insisted on limiting what happened between them to Vegas bothered him. Usually it was he who made those kinds of demands. And despite the fact that he needed the same rules, that their friendship could only survive if they didn't have a repeat performance, a part of him wanted her to want more.

He tightened his arm around her waist and moved closer to the heat of her body, taking what he could before it had to end. She sighed softly in her sleep, obviously dead tired after all the orgasms he'd wrung out of her. Burying his face against her neck, he inhaled the light perfume of cloves and spice mixed with the headier fragrance of sex—with him. His scent was all over her, and he couldn't deny that he liked it. More than was wise.

Tamping down the arousal stirring through him, he absently stroked a hand over her hip and frowned when his palm encountered those scars he'd felt earlier. They weren't fresh wounds, and he had no idea how long she'd had them, but the disturbing fact that she'd hidden the cut marks—or more importantly, that she'd starting cutting again after her stepfather had no longer been a part of her life—concerned him. What had caused her to fall back on that emotional crutch that was so self-destructive, and why hadn't she confided in him?

As best friends, he thought they'd shared everything. She knew all about his shitty past, even the deepest, darkest parts that had too much impact on the man he'd become. And once he'd learned about Katrina's stepfather's abuse, he'd made it his mission to protect the vulnerable girl she'd been. To make sure that no one ever hurt her again. And he'd honestly thought that he'd succeeded in keeping her safe and protected.

These scars, and her reaction tonight when he'd discovered them, indicated otherwise. And while he respected her choice not to talk about them, he hated that something had triggered that past behavior, and for some reason, she hadn't been able to confide in him. He'd been okay dropping the subject tonight, but at some time in the future, he needed to know what had happened and why. Had he failed her? That thought worried and scared him the most.

With those thoughts tumbling through his mind, he stayed with her for another half hour, then decided he needed to leave before he fell asleep, too. As much as he wanted to wake up with her, there was no reason to put the two of them through an awkward morning after. They'd both agreed how tonight would end, and the last thing he wanted to do was get caught sneaking out of her room by Tara or one of his brothers.

Chapter Eight

MASON WAS PRETTY good at multitasking, but even he was having a hard time concentrating on the tattoo he was shading on a client's piece while trying to hear what Katrina found so damn funny. She'd laughed more in the past five minutes than she had since they'd gotten back from Vegas a little over a week ago.

It didn't help his disposition that the person who was responsible for that light, bubbly laughter was a good-looking guy named Blake Cavanaugh, who was a regular client of Caleb's, another one of the artists in the shop. Blake was a suit who co-owned one of the top ad agencies in Chicago—a clean-cut, polished executive by day, but beneath his designer suits, Blake's arms, chest, and back were a canvas of inked art. What was even more irritating was that he was a really nice guy.

CARLY PHILLIPS & ERIKA WILDE

And he had a thing for Katrina. Every time Blake came in to add to his collection of tattoos, he openly flirted with her and asked her out, even though she always gently turned him down. But that didn't stop the guy from turning on the charm, or Katrina from enjoying it, every damn time.

Fucking Romeo, Mason thought irritably.

More amused laughter had Mason gritting his teeth as he applied pressure with the needle in his hand to blend in the slightly different tones of black ink along the raven's wing he was applying on a woman's upper back. He couldn't remember the last time Katrina had been that carefree with him, though he knew for damn sure it had been well before their trip to Vegas for the wedding.

They'd promised to leave their hookup in Vegas, and true to their word, neither one of them had so much as mentioned those two nights together—but Mason thought about them. Constantly. Especially about how Katrina had made him actually *enjoy* sex, as something unique between the two of them. As more than just chasing the physical release and high an orgasm gave him.

Everything they'd done those nights, the playful sexual games, the lengthy foreplay, and making sure that Katrina's pleasure was equal to his own, were all things he never indulged in with other women. Hell, the thought had never crossed his mind before. His own needs had been his sole focus. With Katrina, her feelings mattered, and now anything less seemed shallow and self-serving.

God, he'd never thought it would be this difficult to return home, revert to best friends, and pretend Vegas had never happened. Forgetting was impossible, since he saw Katrina every day at work. Though she *seemed* to be dealing with the situation just fine, he knew better. To the outside world, she was the same Katrina she'd always been—always friendly and smiling, but Mason could feel that things were *off* and, at times, forced and not just with him. And he wasn't sure what to do about it when all he wanted was for things to return to normal.

And he wanted to stop thinking about getting in Katrina's panties again. Yeah, especially that, he thought with a frustrated exhale. No matter how many times he told his dick there wouldn't be a repeat performance, that didn't stop him from wishing and fantasizing.

Finished with the tattoo he'd been applying, he gave the young woman, Rachel, a mirror and let her check the design in her reflection.

"I absolutely love it," Rachel said enthusiastically. "It's exactly what I wanted."

"I always aim to please," Mason drawled, and smiled at her. It was a line he used occasionally with new clients, and it had slipped out automatically. But when she glanced back at him with a seductive look and gave him a once-over, he belatedly realized his mistake.

"Umm, I just bet you do," she murmured flirtatiously, a clear invitation in her gaze.

Before Vegas, this was where he'd work the situation to his advantage and ask her if she wanted to meet up later, but shockingly, the idea just didn't appeal to him. And that said a lot for his state of mind, considering he hadn't been with anyone since that last night with Katrina over a week ago. Normally, by now he would have already moved on to another casual hookup. The fact that he hadn't returned to his regular routine, and even this woman in front of him—who was pretty and curvy and seemingly willing—wasn't tempting him, was a clear indication that his dick wanted what it couldn't have.

Unfortunately, Katrina's hot body was permanently off-limits, and he'd just have to ride out this self-imposed dry spell. At some point—probably when he *stopped* thinking and obsessing about Katrina and comparing every woman to her—his goddamn cock would get back into the game.

So, for one of the very few times in his adult life, he didn't pursue a woman's blatant come-on. Instead, he went over care instructions with her while he applied a layer of antibacterial ointment over the fresh tattoo and covered it with a bandage. As she left his cubicle, Mason glanced over to the front counter, relieved to see that Blake had *finally* left, and Katrina was going over some paperwork with Jasmine, their full-time receptionist. A few moments later, Katrina walked over to the drafting table, where they all did their client drawings and designs, then sat down and started sketching.

He cleaned up his station and decided that in order for him and Katrina to get past this weirdness and set things right between them, they needed to get back to doing some of those typical things they always used to do together as friends. Something light and fun, where they could relax around one another again. And the perfect idea popped into his mind.

Feeling upbeat and hopeful, he checked to make sure his evening was clear of appointments, then strolled over to Katrina. Her head was down as she worked on her design, but she must have seen him in her peripheral vision, because her shoulders tensed. He wanted to reach out and run his hand down her spine until she softened beneath his touch. Hell, he just wanted to touch her, period.

Instead, he leaned casually against the table beside her, watching as she drew a series of cherry blossom vines that entwined around a woman's name. "Is that a commissioned piece?" he asked.

She nodded, her wrist loose as she added a bit of shading to the flowers. "A woman came in earlier and liked one of the exclusive designs in my album and requested a custom piece. She wants cherry blossom vines along her rib cage, incorporating her sister's name. She passed away a few years ago."

A lot of the tattoos they did commemorated a special occasion or were dedicated to a loved one. "Who's doing the ink?"

"Derek," she said, naming the newest artist, who'd

come to work at Inked almost six months ago. "He was the only one who had the day and time free that the client wanted."

Mason continued to quietly watch her draw. She was an incredible artist—always had been, and it was nice to be able to offer their customers a more feminine style of art. Katrina had never had an interest in learning the actual application of a tattoo, but she loved the outlet of creating designs, and he selfishly liked having her in his shop.

She'd been with him since the first day he'd opened the doors to Inked, supporting him and making sure this place ran like a well-oiled machine. She took care of the front end of the shop and paid all the bills. She handled inventory, payroll, and accounting—all the crap that he had no time or interest in doing, not to mention, she kept his personal bills, and his life in general, in order. Just another way that she was so invaluable to him.

After a few minutes of silence, she put down her pencil and glanced up at him, her gaze guarded. "Is there something you need from me, Mason?"

Now *there* was a loaded question if he'd ever heard one. All sorts of innuendos passed through his mind, and he tried hard not to say something stupid and put a damper on what he planned to ask her. "Actually, I was just wondering if you'd like to hang out tonight?"

A slight frown creased her brow. "Hang out?" Her tone was cautious.

"Yeah. Hang out," he said with an easygoing

shrug. "It's been a while and I thought it would be fun to go to Navy Pier. We can ride the Ferris wheel and play some miniature golf and have dinner at Bubba Gump."

The smile that appeared was nostalgic, and Mason knew that she was remembering when they were teenagers and how they'd sneak out on summer nights and spend hours at the pier, staying well after everything shut down. Back then, neither one of them had had any money for the food or attractions, but they'd always managed to have a good time. Being together had been all that mattered—and it had been a bonus that it'd also provided a much-needed escape from their crappy home lives for a few hours.

"It has been a long time," she said wistfully, and Mason thought for sure he'd managed to hook her until she followed that up with, "But I can't tonight. I already have plans."

Her reply was frustratingly vague, when she never used to hesitate to share specific details with him. He waited a few seconds, and when she didn't elaborate as he hoped, he pushed for an answer.

"What kind of plans?" He wanted to know what was more important than spending time with him. Or maybe it was just an excuse not to be alone with him. Whatever the case, he wanted an answer. "What are you doing?"

She hesitated, her teeth grazing her bottom lip in a nervous gesture before she replied. "Well . . . I'm going to dinner with Blake Cavanaugh."

CARLY PHILLIPS & ERIKA WILDE

Her unexpected answer felt like a sucker punch right to the stomach, and it took every ounce of restraint he possessed not to roar like a fucking caveman and drag Katrina off to his office by the hair like said Neanderthal and show her who she belonged to.

Jesus Christ, possessive much? Apparently, when it came to Katrina, he was battling a strong urge to stake his claim, when he had no right to do so.

More calmly than the emotions rioting inside him, he spoke again, "You're going on a date with the guy?" The question scraped across his throat like a sharp knife.

"It's just dinner," she said, as if it was no big deal.

Dinner . . . and then what? Mason wondered. Back to Katrina's place for a nightcap and . . . *Fuck, fuck, fuck,* he couldn't even think of another man touching her without coming unhinged.

"You've spent the past year turning him down," he said, amazed that his voice actually sounded normal. "What changed?"

She sighed softly and tucked the purple ends of her blonde hair behind an ear, which gave him a better view of her beautiful face and the discomfort he saw there. "He's a really nice guy, so why not?"

Mason could give her a dozen reasons *why not*, but he didn't think she'd appreciate his answers: *Because no one will fuck you as well as I do . . .because Cavanaugh has no clue how special you are . . . because you're mine and I can't bear to lose you to another man.*

Yeah, that last one made his goddamn heart *hurt*.

He didn't want any other man to have her, but Mason flat-out didn't have what it took to be the kind of man Katrina needed and deserved. And his biggest fear was that someday she'd realize that, even as a friend, Mason wasn't worth her while. That had been a familiar pattern in his youth—a mother who didn't give a shit and chose drugs over her kids, a father who didn't even know he existed, teachers who never tried to understand the source of his belligerent attitude and instead wrote him off as a loser. Which had only pushed him to be even more of a delinquent, because why the hell not? He'd had absolutely nothing to lose.

A part of him even knew that those doubts about himself were the reason he didn't let his relationships last longer than a one-night stand. If he didn't let anyone close enough to affect his feelings—Katrina being the one exception—there was no risk of rejection. His detached attitude had always served him well and kept his emotions isolated. Other than his brothers, Katrina was the one person he'd allowed himself to care for, and if he couldn't give her *all* of himself, did he really have the right to stand in her way of finding that with someone else?

Jesus, his stomach churned and he seriously felt as though he was going to throw up. Because he knew the answer to that question, and he had to *stop* being a selfish asshole when it came to her. And that meant he needed to face the reality of Katrina moving on with another man who wasn't as screwed up as he was, and who would love her wholeheartedly and without any fears or reservations.

"You're right," he finally said, even as everything within him rebelled at his acceptance of the situation. "Blake is a nice guy. Have a good time on your date."

And then Mason walked away while trying to convince himself that he'd done the right thing for Katrina, even if it felt so damn wrong.

KATRINA PULLED HER iridescent purple Volkswagen Beetle into a just-vacated parking spot on the street near Antico, a higher-end Italian restaurant in Bucktown, where she was meeting Blake Cavanaugh. Part of her stipulation for having dinner with him was that she drove her own car and met him at the restaurant so that they could leave separately, as well. Mason might be under the impression that she was out on a date tonight, but that wasn't the case at all.

She'd agreed to see Blake after hours for one reason only, and that's because he'd said he had a business proposition to present to her, and she was curious enough to find out what that proposal entailed. She'd already made the difficult decision to find another job, and she was actively looking and keeping her prospects open while training Jasmine at Inked to take on more responsibilities so it would be a smoother transition when Katrina left.

Enduring Mason's presence every single day, for

up to ten hours, was taking its toll. Emotionally, her heart ached in a way she'd never experienced before. She knew in order to save their friendship, she needed space because it was just too hard and painful to watch every move he made at the shop, along with watching him flirt with women on a regular basis. The jealousy would eventually eat her alive.

Bottom line, she couldn't move on with her life the way she needed to with the way things currently were. And especially after the weekend she'd spent with Mason in Vegas. Those two nights had changed everything for her, and nothing for him. Then again, he hadn't made her any promises, and she'd known up front that's how he operated when it came to women and sex. But that knowledge didn't make what she felt for Mason any less painful.

Pushing thoughts of Mason from her mind so she could focus on Blake's proposition, whatever it might be, she got out of her car, engaged the alarm, and made her way across the street. She'd gone home after work and changed into a nice pair of black cigarette pants and a dark purple off-the-shoulder blouse that matched the highlights in her hair, and a funky pair of heeled pumps that looked as though someone had spattered them with purple paint. The outfit was nicer than the casual attire she wore at Inked, and more appropriate for what Katrina considered a business dinner—*not* a date.

When she reached Antico, she found Blake waiting outside for her.

His appreciative gaze took in her changed appearance, and he grinned. "Wow, I thought you looked great today, but tonight, you look stunning."

She smiled and accepted the compliment gracefully. "Thank you."

Despite *her* being all about business tonight, she knew Blake would try and mix in a bit of pleasure. He'd been very clear about his romantic interest in her, and the man was charming and persuasive, but Katrina was determined to keep things professional.

As they walked into the restaurant, she noticed that he'd gone home and changed, too. He now wore a pair of black slacks and a dark gray long-sleeved dress shirt. He'd forgone a tie and suit jacket, and while he looked much more casual, there was no mistaking that this man still had the ability to command whatever room he walked into. He just had that kind of self-assured presence.

On the outside, he was a clean-cut, good-looking man with chiseled features and dark brown eyes that shone with confidence and intelligence. But she knew that beneath those layers of clothes, he was a tattooed bad boy. It was such a contradiction, and while Katrina couldn't deny that those dual sides to Blake's personality were sexy as hell, that's as far as her fascination went. It really was too bad she couldn't return his interest, not when her heart belonged to someone else. Even if that *someone else* didn't have a damn clue.

Which was why she needed to put distance between her and Mason, so she could learn to live without him in her life every single day. And then, maybe some guy would come along and fill that void in a more permanent way. After seeing the love and affection that Samantha and Clay shared, she wanted a man to cherish her. She wanted to get married and create a family of her own. She didn't want to settle for less than the whole package.

They stepped up to the podium to check in for their reservation, but as soon as the twenty-something girl saw Blake, her eyes lit up and she smiled brightly, clearly recognizing him as a regular.

"Hi, Mr. Cavanaugh," she greeted him, and didn't bother to look at Katrina. "Your table is ready."

"Excellent." The hostess walked into the restaurant, and Blake settled his big hand on Katrina's lower back as they followed the girl.

It was a gentlemanly gesture, and while Katrina thought she might feel some kind of spark of awareness or even a flutter or attraction, it just didn't happen, and she knew it wouldn't, with any man, until she was over Mason. God, she hoped that was even possible.

They sat down at a table in a quiet, private corner, and as soon as the waiter arrived, Blake ordered a bottle of wine for the two of them. Katrina assumed it had to be expensive, because she'd never heard of it before, and Blake didn't look like the kind of guy who drank cheap Chardonnay. She perused her menu of Italian fare and he did the same.

CARLY PHILLIPS & ERIKA WILDE

After a few minutes, Blake gave her his suggestions. "The roasted duck is fabulous, and so is the smoked pork shoulder ragù."

She wrinkled her nose and peeked at him over her menu, knowing she was about to admit to her very boring and generic palate, versus his more refined one. "I'm sorry to disappoint you, but I can't bring myself to eat a duck, and a pork shoulder just sounds . . . wrong."

He chuckled. "Okay, then."

At least he was amused by her lack of sophistication when it came to food. "I mean, this is an Italian restaurant," she pointed out. "Don't they have ravioli or plain ol' spaghetti and meatballs?"

His gaze glimmered with more laughter. "Sounds like I should have taken you to the Olive Garden."

"Oh, my God, I *love* the Olive Garden," she said enthusiastically.

"I'll make a note of that for next time," he said, and put his own menu aside. "In the meantime, I think you'll enjoy the Tagliatelle Bolognese, which is long ribbons of pasta in a meat-based sauce. It's as close to spaghetti as you're going to get," he said with a grin.

She flashed him a satisfied smile. "Perfect."

The waiter arrived with the wine and poured each of them a glass, then came back with a basket of bread and butter. He took their individual orders—Blake went with the braised short ribs—and once the server left them alone again, Katrina directed their conversation toward why she was really there.

"So, what is this business proposition you have for me?" she asked.

"What? No small talk first?" His voice was once again infused with humor.

At least he didn't take things too seriously, which made him extremely charismatic and likeable. "Tell you what," she said as she reached for a piece of bread and slathered it with butter. "Let's get the business stuff out of the way, and then if there's time, we'll do some small talk."

He absently swirled his white wine in his glass. "Sounds naughty."

"I think that's *pillow* talk," she corrected him, and took a bite of the bread.

"I can't get anything past you, can I?" He shook his head in mock disappointment.

"No, I'm pretty sharp like that," she teased.

He took a drink of his wine and then sat back in his chair, his pose relaxed but still very much in control. "Okay, here's the deal. You know that I co-own an ad agency, right?"

She nodded as she finished her slice of bread and reached for another—dang, she was hungry, and she wasn't one of those skinny women who wouldn't eat bread or a bowl of pasta in front of a man. Not wanting to talk with her mouth full, she made the universal sound for *yes*. "Mmm hmm." She also knew that Cavanaugh and Zimmerman was a very reputable agency, and judging by the designer clothes he wore and the sports car he drove, the firm wasn't doing too shabby.

"Well, we're a full-service agency that has a design department," he explained. "We currently have an opening for a junior graphic designer who would work directly under the senior director of the art department."

She took a drink of her wine—and yeah, the quality was outstanding—then tipped her head to the side. "And how does this pertain to me?"

"I thought it might be something that you'd be interested in," he said seriously.

"Why me?" Her eyes rounded in surprise. "I don't know anything about advertising. Well, that's not completely true," she amended. "I've done some marketing for Inked, but that's hardly the kind of experience I'm sure you're looking for or need."

He leaned forward in his chair and braced his arms on the table, his gaze direct. "We want to hire someone with a fresh perspective and enthusiasm. Someone who isn't trained and will think outside the box when it comes to creative designs for our clients."

As exciting as the opportunity sounded, she still didn't understand how she fit into that way of thinking. Wouldn't they at least want someone with a degree? "Blake . . .I didn't go to college, and I've never worked for a big company. I'm pretty good with Photoshop and a few other graphic design programs, but I'm not sure that's enough for an ad agency as big or reputable as yours."

He smiled. "Sweetheart, I wouldn't be sitting here

asking if you'd be interested in the job if I didn't think you were a good fit for Cavanaugh and Zimmerman. Would I like to go out on a date with you? Absolutely. But one has nothing to do with the other. Right now, at this moment, my interest in you is all business. I don't want you to think that one thing hinges on the other. And from what I know and have seen, you are more than enough for what we want as a junior graphic designer."

Just as he finished his comment, their meals arrived, and yes, her fancy Tagliatelle Bolognese did resemble something that looked like an Italian meal to her. The waiter grated fresh parmesan over her pasta, refilled their wineglasses, and once Blake assured him that everything was great, the guy moved on to another table.

Once their server was gone and they were alone again, Katrina asked a question she was very curious about. "So, what do you know about me and what have you seen to give you the indication that I'd be a good fit for your agency?" If she was even going to consider this proposition, then she needed to be reassured that he really did know her strengths and limitations in regard to the position he was offering.

"Good question," he said, seemingly impressed with her inquiry as he cut into a braised short rib. "I've been coming to Inked for over six months now. As for what I know about you, Caleb has been very talkative during my many sessions, and he's answered a lot of my questions about you. According to him, you're the reason the shop runs as smoothly as it does, so that tells me you've got a great work ethic. And I've watched you in action with other customers and how you manage the shop while I'm there, too."

"Stalker much?" she teased.

He chuckled as he took a bite of the vegetables accompanying his meat. "It's called scoping out a potential prospect."

She twirled her strands of pasta around her fork. "Managing a tattoo shop has nothing to do with working for an ad agency."

"True, but I know that you're someone who will always strive to better herself, and those are the kinds of qualities that are important in the people I hire." He hesitated for a moment as he drank his wine, then continued. "What I've also seen is your freehand artwork, in your personal album and what's pinned on the gallery wall in the shop. Every time I come in, I look to see what you've done that's new. And every time, I'm impressed as hell with your designs and creativity."

She glanced down at her plate, her face warming at the thought of how thoroughly he'd been analyzing her as a potential employee for his agency. And she suddenly had a bout of insecurities. "I'm just not sure that my art and designs at Inked will translate to what you need for an ad agency."

"*I'm* sure, and that's all that matters," he said confidently. "I'm known for bringing in untrained and inexperienced employees when I see the kind of talent that meshes well with our agency. I've rarely been wrong about the people I've handpicked to hire. In fact, most of those employees have become the backbone of the company and are the ones who are continually bringing a new and fresh perspective to ad campaigns and marketing ideas."

Despite her slight concerns about not having any experience in the field, she found that the idea was starting to tempt her. "You're so damn persuasive," she said with a shake of her head.

He shrugged unapologetically. "I know what I want, and I'm pretty determined about getting my way if it's important enough."

She couldn't help but feel flattered—that he believed so unconditionally in her ability to fit in so well with his company. They finished their dinners, and after the waiter cleared away their dishes, Blake glanced across the table and met her gaze.

"So, what do you think?" he asked.

She exhaled a deep breath. The offer was incredibly generous, exciting even, but it was also so unexpected. Without a doubt, she knew that finding a new job was imperative to her friendship with Mason, and her heart and emotions, but she'd never been one to jump into something without really thinking things through.

"I really appreciate your job offer, and I'm very interested," she said respectfully. "But I can't give you a definite decision right this second."

"I don't expect you to." His tone was understanding. "Take a week and think about everything I've said, and consider the growth and opportunities with an ad agency that is one of the top ten firms in Chicago. And I know we didn't discuss pay, but I promise I'll make it worth your while."

"Thank you," she said appreciatively, realizing there really was no downside to taking the job. Even still, she'd take the one-week time frame to make sure a new career in advertising was what she really wanted.

"So, enough business," he said in a more upbeat tone as a sexy smile curved his lips. "I'm more interested in getting to the pillow talk."

Of course he was. Playing along, she leaned forward in her chair and whispered in a provocative voice, "Want to know *my* version of seductive pillow talk?"

He angled closer, too, his eyes a deep, dark brown as he stared intently at her. "Absolutely," he murmured.

She closed her eyes, slowly licked her lips, then opened them again and teased him. "I *need* chocolate dessert." She sighed and smiled mischievously. "That's about as hot as pillow talk gets for me."

He laughed and shook his head. "I'm not about to deprive any woman of having dessert. Besides, it's a win-win situation. You get to eat it, and I get to watch."

As long as he didn't *touch*, they were all good.

Chapter Nine

MASON SAT ALONE at the far end of the bar at Kincaid's and nursed a bottle of Sam Adams while debating if he should move on to something stronger so he'd stop thinking about Katrina on her *dat*e with Blake, and what they might be doing. If the guy was kissing her, touching her, making a move on her . . . *Fuck.* The troubling thought made him want to plant his fist into something hard to release some of the pent-up frustration building inside him.

"Well, this is a first," Mason heard his brother, Levi, drawl just before he sat down in the vacant chair next to his.

"*What's* a first?" Mason asked irritably, in no mood for his younger brother's goody-two-shoes commentary.

"You sitting at a bar all by yourself and looking quite pathetic," Levi said, sounding far too amused at

CARLY PHILLIPS & ERIKA WILDE

the situation.

"Well, you could always fuck off," Mason suggested, then finished his beer.

"I could," Levi said, his tone more amused than offended. "But seeing you like this is much more fun."

Mason glared at his brother. He'd come to Kincaid's because he'd stupidly thought he could wallow in his misery alone. Mason had known for certain that Clay wouldn't be here. Now that Clay was domesticated by marriage, he spent more time at the new home he'd purchased for himself and Samantha, instead of at the bar. Levi didn't drink alcohol and usually didn't show up at the bar unless there was a specific reason, and Mason resented Levi butting into what should have been a private pity party. No smartasses invited or allowed. Obviously, Levi had missed that particular memo.

"What are you doing here?" Mason asked testily.

His belligerent attitude didn't so much as faze Levi, who, as a beat cop, was used to dealing with far more intimidating criminals. "Well, I was watching *House of Cards* on Netflix at home, and I got a concerned text from Tara telling me that something was seriously wrong with you and I needed to get over here ASAP."

"Sorry to tear you away from an exciting night in front of the TV," Mason said sarcastically. "But there's nothing wrong and you made a trip down here for nothing."

Levi leaned an arm on the counter. "Well, considering you aren't taking advantage of all the single women here tonight, and you aren't off screwing one of them already, I'd have to agree with Tara. Are you sick? Do you have a fever? Or has your dick finally become discriminate? You know, that big word we talked about on the plane ride to Vegas that means you've actually gotten particular about where that dick goes, and with whom?"

Levi didn't have to say the name *Katrina*, because his brother wasn't stupid, or a fool. Jesus, he hated when Levi did that—how his brother silently sat back and didn't miss a goddamn thing going on around him. Even as a kid, Levi had been quiet and introverted, but incredibly attuned to everything. As an adult, it was fucking unnerving to have all that intensity focused on him.

Resisting the urge to flip Levi the middle finger, Mason gave him a tight smile instead. "My dick is *fine*; thank you very much for your concern."

He hoped that Levi would take the hint and go back home. Instead, he caught Tara's attention and motioned her over to the end of the bar.

"I told you it was bad," Tara said once she arrived, her concerned gaze bouncing from Mason to Levi.

"Jesus Christ," Mason snapped indignantly. "I'm fucking *fine*."

"He's so not fine," Levi said with a sympathetic shake of his head. "He'll take another Sam's, and I'll take the usual."

"You got it," Tara said, and moved away to get their drinks.

She returned a few minutes later, setting a fresh bottle of beer in front of Mason and a tall glass that contained a nonalcoholic orange spritzer on Levi's napkin.

Mason glanced at his brother's pansy-ass drink. "I wish that someone would spike your fucking orange juice. I'd love to see you get drunk. Just once."

Levi smirked and took a long drink of his mixture of orange juice and soda water. "Not gonna happen," he said as he set his glass back down on the counter. "I have no desire to ever drink alcohol and do stupid shit."

Getting drunk and doing stupid shit was pretty much the sum of Mason's teenage years and some of his adult ones, too. "Why not?" he asked curiously.

Levi shrugged. "It's a control thing," he said vaguely.

Mason was pretty sure Levi's reasons all tied into their childhood, and how each one of them dealt with their horrible situation in very different ways. Levi *did* like to be in control. He was calm, focused, and composed. Always had been. Growing up, Mason used to hate how nothing seemed to affect Levi, but he'd learned over the years that his brother's quiet personality was Levi's way of coping with all the emotional upheaval in their lives.

While Levi internalized their painful situation, Mason had gone to the opposite extreme and let his rage drive him toward every act of rebellion that came his way. It wasn't until Mason was older that he'd learned to control those angry outbursts.

"So, do you want to talk about it?" Levi asked, interrupting his thoughts.

Mason frowned at his brother. "It?"

Levi rolled his eyes. "Katrina," he said more specifically.

Mason's first instinct was to play stupid and say, "What about Katrina?" but he was so damn tired of denying his feelings for his best friend. Everything about their current situation was eating him alive inside, and one of the very few people he trusted was his brother. Levi wasn't one to judge, and right now, that's exactly what Mason needed—someone to listen and hopefully offer some helpful advice.

"Katrina and I slept together in Vegas," Mason said before he lost the nerve.

"Yeah, I figured," Levi said as he ran his thumb and forefinger along the condensation gathering on his glass.

"How did you 'figure'?" Mason asked, curious to know what had given him and Katrina away.

Levi laughed. "Are you serious? The moment you carried Katrina out of Coyote Ugly like a goddamn caveman, both Clay and I knew that things were going to come to a head between you two. Both of you have been skirting around your attraction for years, but lately, the sexual tension has been pretty intense. Between Katrina dancing up on the bar and you getting all territorial about other men touching her, it was bound to get heated. And considering how

CARLY PHILLIPS & ERIKA WILDE

awkward and weird things were with the two of you the next day at the wedding, it was a no-brainer that you guys had sex."

Mason frowned. "You were there when I told Tara that nothing happened."

"And *she* believed you, but I'm your brother and I know when you're lying. I can see it in your eyes, especially when it comes to Katrina. And being a cop makes it even easier to spot when you're not being totally honest."

"Nice," Mason muttered. He'd have to remember *not* to look his brother in the eyes the next time he was telling a fib.

"So, you slept together," Levi said, bringing the conversation back to the issue at hand. "What's the problem?"

"The problem is, I totally fucked up the friendship. No pun intended," he muttered.

A slight smile touched the corner of Levi's mouth. "How so?"

"Because now things are . . . different between us." He dragged his fingers through his hair in aggravation. "Awkward, weird, and tense, even though we agreed at the time that it wouldn't be. And she's out on a date with another guy tonight, and it's driving me nuts thinking about it."

Levi's brows rose in surprise. "Are you saying that you're actually jealous of who Katrina is seeing and dating?"

His stomach churned with acid. "Yeah, and I fucking hate it." He'd never had an issue with who she'd dated in the past, but that had been before they'd blurred the lines of their friendship. Now that he knew what it felt like to be inside of her, to have her body wrapped so intimately around his, for the first time ever with a woman, it changed everything.

Levi absently swirled his orange juice in his glass as he thought for a moment. Then he glanced at Mason with a crooked smile "You know, I don't understand why the two of you don't just start dating like a normal couple."

Mason frowned. "Because I don't *date*. And because . . .because she's my best friend and that's just . . . weird."

Levi laughed. "Dude, you had *sex* with her. And you're worried about *dating* Katrina being weird?"

"I know, I know," he said, realizing how ridiculous it all sounded. But he couldn't stop those doubts from continually rearing their ugly head, and he let them out before he lost the nerve.

"I've never dated anyone before. Ever," he said as he peeled at the label on his beer so he didn't have to look directly at Levi while confessing his greatest fears. "And I'm so afraid I'll fuck up everything worse with Katrina than it already is. What if I screw up and then we don't even have the friendship to fall back on and I lose her forever?" *God, that would destroy him.* "What if she realizes that I'm just not that great of a guy and she could do so much better? That I'm a total loser who doesn't have the ability to offer her everything she needs from that kind of relationship?"

"If you were a loser, she wouldn't have stuck with you for the past twelve years," Levi said in a wry tone.

"As a *friend*," Mason corrected his brother. "Not as someone who wants something . . . *more*."

Understanding glimmered in Levi's gaze. "Look, you don't know how things will play out unless you *try* to build something more with Katrina."

Mason swallowed hard before admitting the truth. "I'm afraid."

"You can't let the past keep defining your future actions," Levi stated bluntly. "At some point, you need to change your pattern of behavior in order for anything else around you to change."

Mason narrowed his gaze at his brother. "And what actions are those?"

"You being a manwhore," Levi said, obviously trying to inject some humor into the conversation. In the next few seconds, his expression turned much more serious. "You think I don't understand why you don't let any one woman close enough for you to fall in love?"

There Levi went again, being all observant and perceptive, though Mason was curious to know what conclusions his brother had drawn. "Why don't you enlighten me with your wisdom?" he drawled.

Levi ignored his smartass tone. "We grew up with a mother who, for all intents and purposes, abandoned the kids she'd never wanted anyway, and all three of us dealt with that situation in very different ways. Clay became the parent. The responsible one who made sure we stayed together. Even though it meant he had to work his ass off in order to give us a decent life without the constant abuse of Wyatt," he said of their mother's asshole boyfriend who'd taken great enjoyment in terrorizing them, until one day Clay had fought back.

Thank God that part of their past was done, gone, and finished. And even though Wyatt had recently come back into their lives to threaten Clay once more, it hadn't ended well for Wyatt, who was now in jail for a murder he'd committed over a year ago. But at least that confrontation had allowed Clay to finally open himself up to the possibility of a future with Samantha. What would it take for Mason to believe in himself that way?

Levi continued on. "I was so young, but even I developed my own coping mechanisms. I would always . . ." He frowned and let the words go unsaid, as if he didn't want to shine that particular mirror on himself and reflect on his own painful memories. And Mason wasn't about to push him for more.

"*You* were a goddamn hellion," Levi said instead, turning things back to Mason. "After everything we went through, with our mother going to jail and Wyatt giving up on us thanks to Clay, I remember you doing everything you could to push Clay to the breaking point. It was like you were continually testing him, and he never gave up on you. Ever."

"I know," Mason said, and he was grateful, because he hadn't made it easy on his older brother at all.

"So, this thing you do with women . . . You don't form attachments because you're hung up on what happened in the past," Levi said. "You walk away without even trying to see if something other than sex might develop, and you deliberately choose women who aren't going to want anything more than something physical so there's no threat of you getting emotionally involved. But Katrina . . . she's different from all those casual encounters. She always has been."

Mason couldn't argue with Levi's theory because it was the truth.

"That's why you've always kept Katrina in the best friend zone," Levi went on while Mason digested everything he had to say. Things he knew but rarely verbalized or liked to think about. "Because that way, you can keep Katrina close and not worry about doing something stupid to make her leave you. But that's what best friends do. They stick around during the tough times, they support you and always have your back. And they forgive you when you're an asshole."

That last part made Mason chuckle. "And we all know that's happened a time or two."

"Or a dozen," Levi added with a smirk. "My best advice? Don't be *that* asshole and repeat your hit-it-and-quit-it pattern with Katrina and give her a reason to put any more distance between the two of you. This is your chance to get things right with her, and the fact that you came back from Vegas and haven't reverted to your manwhore ways tells me that maybe she's the one. Hell, maybe she's always been the one and you're just now opening yourself up to the possibility."

As scary as that sounded, Mason nodded in agreement. That's exactly what it felt like—like he was finally allowing himself to be emotionally vulnerable for the first time in his life, but he had no idea where Katrina stood. For all he knew, she'd already moved on to Blake, and her time with Mason in Vegas was nothing more than a distant memory.

He swore beneath his breath, refusing to even consider that possibility. Nor was he going to let some other guy get between him and Katrina. Not without a fight.

Mason glanced at Levi, curious about a few things his brother had left unsaid. "So, since you've psychoanalyzed me, how come you've never had a serious relationship before?"

"Who says I haven't?" Levi shot back.

His brother's quick reply caught Mason by surprise. "Well, considering I've never seen you date a woman for any length of time, either, or bring one around for Clay and me to meet, I just thought you were being *discriminate*. See, I know what that big word means," Mason joked. "Or maybe you're saving yourself for marriage."

Levi laughed out loud. "Not even close. I'm just more discreet than you."

Mason watched his brother finish the rest of his orange juice spritzer and push the glass across the bar.

Levi had gone through all of high school without a girlfriend—that Mason knew of—and right after graduating at the age of seventeen, he'd joined the Army with Clay's consent and served in the military for four years. He'd been back for over two years, and was now a cop with Chicago P.D., and there was no woman in his life to speak of.

"Were you seeing someone in the military?" Mason asked, wondering if something had happened during that time.

"Tonight was all about you, not me," Levi said, smoothly skirting the issue as he stood up and clapped Mason on the back. "My intervention here is done, and now I can get back to *House of Cards* with a clear conscience, knowing I saved my brother from doing something stupid that he might regret later. Oh, and no charge for the therapy session."

"Here's your payment," Mason said, and gave Levi the middle finger.

Levi just shook his head and chuckled as he headed out of the bar, leaving Mason alone once again. But at least this time he wasn't wallowing. No, now he was strategizing and thinking about a game plan to win over the one woman—*the only woman*—he wanted in his life.

✧　✧　✧

WHEN MASON ARRIVED at the shop the following morning at ten a.m., he was feeling upbeat and optimistic about Katrina and the day ahead, despite the fact that she'd gone to dinner with another man the night before. He carried a to-go drink tray with two large coffees he'd stopped and picked up on the way to work—a straight black brew for him and Katrina's preferred steamed caramel latte—along with her favorite apple-and-cream-cheese Danish.

As he stepped into Inked, he was greeted by the sight of a dozen red roses on the front counter in a crystal vase and Katrina standing there in a cute black mini-dress and lace-up thigh-high boots he immediately fantasized about having wrapped around his waist while he fucked her against the counter. Yeah, his dick supported that idea one hundred percent.

She had a big smile on her face . . . but it wasn't for him. No, it was a result of the small card she was reading that had come with the flowers that Blake had no doubt sent.

So much for surprising her with a coffee and pastry. His meager gifts were no match for the vibrant, gorgeous arrangement that had probably cost a small fortune. Clearly, Blake was staking his claim, and Mason exhaled a deep, calming breath so he didn't overreact and say something *stupid* that would just cause Katrina to withdraw from him even more. His goal was the opposite, to reestablish the friendship that meant so much to both of them, and build from there.

But Jesus, he hadn't expected to have to compete with wealth and sophistication and a guy who knew how to woo and romance a woman. Those were skills Mason had never had a need for, but he realized that he definitely needed to step up his game if he was going to compete with someone of Blake Cavanaugh's caliber.

He came up beside Katrina, and she quickly stuffed the card she was reading back into the envelope before he could see what it said. She buried it into her purse that was still on the counter, then turned around to face him with a flush on her cheeks and her expression flustered.

From reading Blake's note, he wondered? Shit. He hated that another man could have that effect on her. Jealousy tightened across his chest, and he refused to allow his mind to conjure up images of Blake and Katrina together, doing those *things* that only Mason wanted the privilege of doing with and to her.

"Hey," she said with a forced smile, her demeanor reserved, as if she wasn't sure what to expect from him this morning.

"Hey, yourself," he replied with a *genuine* smile while doing his best not to act like a possessive dick, which would only put her guard up even more. "I got you a caramel latte and a Danish," he said, handing her both.

"Thank you," she said, this time sounding truly pleased by the thoughtful gesture.

He tossed the to-go holder in the trash and took a sip of his strong coffee. "How was your date with Blake last night?" *See, he could totally be civilized about the situation.*

"It was . . . good," she said, much too vaguely, and wouldn't quite meet his gaze.

What the hell did *good* mean? Mason didn't push. Wouldn't push. But fuck, he wanted to. Badly. So, instead, he said, "I'm glad you had a good time," then headed over to his station to set up for his first appointment of the day.

When he casually glanced back to the front counter, he caught Katrina watching him with a frown as she took a bite of her pastry. Obviously, she hadn't expected him to act so rationally, and even Mason had to admit he was impressed with himself because it had taken every ounce of control he possessed not to carry her off to his private office and put his stamp of ownership all over her the best way *he* knew how.

Fuck expensive roses. Mason was all about making sure he staked his claim in a more memorable way. Whether Katrina knew it or not, she was his. And he was going to do everything in his power to prove it.

Chapter Ten

K ATRINA WALKED INTO her apartment and set her purse and keys on the small table by the door, then headed into her bedroom to change out of the dress and boots she'd worn to work. It had been a long, busy day, and it hadn't helped matters that every time she'd seen the vase of roses sitting on the front counter she'd thought about Blake's job offer. No doubt, that had been his intent.

And then there was Mason and his strange behavior. He'd arrived at the shop in a good mood, with her favorite breakfast items in hand, and it had felt like a peace offering between them, which she'd welcomed. And even though he'd seen the flowers and asked very nicely about her *date* with Blake, she'd wished that he'd exhibited even a small amount of jealousy. Something, anything, to give her some kind of indication that he might have more than just *best friend* feelings for her.

"And if he did, then what?" she muttered to herself as she sat on the bed, unlaced her boots, and pulled them off. Mason didn't know the meaning of monogamous, and she was a one-man kind of woman. End of story.

After slipping out of her dress and bra, she put on a soft, cotton camisole and a pair of comfortable sleep shorts, then padded into the kitchen to make something for dinner. She opened the refrigerator and perused the meager contents. Geez, she should have stopped at the grocery store on the way home. Or at least picked up some kind of takeout.

"Okay, scrambled eggs it is," she said to herself since her choices were limited. Just as she started to reach into the fridge to grab the carton, the doorbell rang.

She headed back to the entryway and looked through the peephole and saw Mason standing on the other side—reminiscent of that last night in Vegas when he'd come to her room. The memory of what had happened once she'd let him inside made her traitorous heart flutter. She had no idea what he was doing there, or what he wanted, but she couldn't ignore the fact that he was there. He had to have seen her car parked in her spot.

When she opened the door, she was greeted with the delicious aroma from the pizza box he was holding in one hand, which was from their favorite pizzeria. In his other hand, he was carrying a paper sack from the grocery store.

The savory scent of the pie made her stomach growl, and he grinned, even as he blatantly took in her camisole and shorts with a heated gaze that made her breasts tingle. "Sausage, mushroom, and olives," he said, indicating he'd brought a pizza with her favorite toppings. "I hope you haven't eaten dinner yet."

This wasn't the first time he'd showed up at her place unannounced and with food, and it just felt so . . . normal. Like old times, and she couldn't resist—even as she wondered why he was there after a week and a half of tension between them.

Stepping back, she let him into her apartment, then led the way to the kitchen. "Actually, you saved me from a boring meal of scrambled eggs. That pizza smells amazing."

He placed the cardboard box on the counter, along with the grocery bag, then began taking things out of the sack. "Here's some root beer to wash it all down with, and some Ben and Jerry's Salted Caramel Core ice cream to go with the movie I rented from Redbox for us to watch," he said as he put the pint into the freezer.

She leaned back against the counter, suddenly feeling . . . overwhelmed. And so confused. This scenario was like a flashback to some of the best times she'd spent with Mason—eating pizza, then gorging on her favorite ice cream while watching a scary flick. Which had always included cuddling with him on the couch because she had a love/hate relationship with thrillers and inevitably clung to Mason during the gory parts, or buried her face against his neck.

But all that had been *before*, and now she didn't know what to make of all *this*. And his changed behavior. Especially after how strained things had been between them for the past week and a half.

"Mason, what are you doing here?" she blurted out.

He set the plates that he'd just taken down from the cupboard on the counter, then walked toward her, the territorial gleam in his blue eyes making her pulse race. Everything seemed to change in that moment—his cheerful demeanor shifting to something far more arousing.

When he reached her, he braced his hands on either side of where she was standing and leaned in close enough for her breasts to brush across his chest—making her shiver and her nipples tighten almost painfully.

"I'm staking my claim, Kitty-Kat," he said, his words as possessive as the rumbling sound of his voice. "*That's* what I'm doing here."

She opened her mouth, then shut it, stunned by his words. She'd been expecting him to say something along the lines of "*I'm here to get our friendship back on track,*" not that he planned to pursue her or *stake his claim*. While her body was willing to let him mark her however he pleased, her heart and mind were far more practical about his declaration.

"I don't want to be your convenient fuck buddy," she said, hating the hint of doubt that crept into her voice, but she couldn't help how she felt. "Or be another notch on your belt."

"That's not what I want, either. I swear it. I want you. Only you," he said as he placed his hands on her waist and pressed his hips to hers. He flashed her a charming grin that belied the sudden hint of nerves in his gaze. "And to prove it, I'm getting a brand new belt with *your* name on it, and while I definitely want to fuck you again, it won't be as your *buddy*."

She swallowed hard as she tried to digest everything, especially the fact that he was implying that he wanted them to be an exclusive couple, when Mason didn't do relationships. Ever.

She shook her head in confusion. "I don't understand . . . "

"I'm having a hard time understanding all this, too," he admitted honestly. "But there is one thing I know with absolute certainty, and that is that I can't stand the thought of another man touching you. Not after everything that happened in Vegas. You went out with Blake last night, and I was so fucking miserable and jealous it nearly gave me an ulcer. And then those goddamn flowers that I had to look at all day today . . . " His words trailed off and he clenched his jaw in irritation. "I assume Blake sent them?"

She nodded. "Yes." But what Mason didn't know was that the note Blake had attached hadn't been romantic at all, but rather a nice message about how he hoped she'd become a part of the Cavanaugh and Zimmerman team.

Mason frowned at her, and his hands tightened on her waist. "If Blake had been around, I can guarantee that we would have come to blows over you, and *I* would have won."

She looked at him in surprise. "I had no idea you were jealous."

His expression turned adorably sheepish. "Because I was *trying* not to be an asshole about the situation, and it was damn hard." He stared into her eyes, his gaze searching hers. "Just tell me one thing. Do I *need* to be worried or jealous about Blake?"

"No," she said, automatically honest in return. Romantically speaking, there was no interest or attraction. But Katrina wasn't ready to share her job offer with Mason, not until she made some kind of decision, one way or the other.

He exhaled a relieved breath. "Good."

She bit her bottom lip, knowing that she had her own concerns to express, and she was still honest-to-God floored at the direction of their conversation. This was Mason. *Mason*, coming to her asking her for a chance. It was everything she'd ever hoped for or dreamed about except . . .

"Do I need to worry about . . . other women?" It was a fair question, considering his track record, and she needed that reassurance.

"No, you don't have to worry about other women," he replied, his voice sincere, then the corner of his mouth lifted in a wry grin. "I haven't been with anyone but you since before Vegas. My dick doesn't want anyone *but* you, Kitty-Kat."

She laughed lightly, even as the cynical part of her brain whispered the question, *for how long?* "Umm, that's so . . . romantic?"

"It's the truth." He lifted his hands and framed her face in his palms, the warmth and affection in his gaze unmistakable. "I want this to be so different with you, but this is unchartered territory for me. Can we just take it slow and easy and see where it goes?"

He wasn't asking for forever, not that Katrina had expected him to considering this was all new to him. And because she was well aware that there were no guarantees in any of this, she also knew exactly what was at risk—her emotions, and the potential for heartbreak if Mason decided he wasn't cut out for a committed relationship. Not to mention ruining their friendship, which she cherished and meant so much to her.

But she also knew if she didn't take this chance with him, she'd always look back and regret it, as well as wonder what if. She'd loved this man for so many years, and for the first time in his life, he was trying to open himself up to a deeper, closer, more intimate relationship, which took time. *Time* he was willing to invest in a relationship with her. Something he'd never, ever done before for another woman, and she couldn't deny that she was going into this cautious and guarded.

"You're looking at me with those big, wide eyes, and I have no idea what you're thinking," he said as he stroked his thumbs along her cheek, making her realize how long she'd been silent—obviously long enough to make him worry. "But I need you to say *yes*, that you'll give me a chance."

This time, she didn't hesitate. "Yes," she said, and a rush of excitement zipped through her at the thought of being his.

A release of breath escaped him as he pulled her mouth up to his and kissed her, so slow and deep and sweet it made her ache. He slid one of his hands into her hair and pressed his lower body into hers while tracing her lips with his tongue before sweeping back inside. Beneath the zipper of his jeans, he was hard and thick, all for her.

The knowledge thrilled her, and she melted against him while pushing her palms beneath the hem of his T-shirt so she could touch the hard, muscular plane of his stomach. What she wanted even more was to lick her way down his chest and drag her tongue lower, until she was kneeling on the floor and had his shaft between her lips.

Excited by the thought, she tugged on the button securing his jeans, but he caught her wrists and stopped her before she could get inside. He ended the hot kiss and stared down at her while pressing her palm to the outline of his erection.

"Fuck," he breathed as she squeezed him tightly through the denim. "That's what *you* do to me, Kitty-Kat."

She liked how that sounded. Loved that she had

the ability to make him so hard and eager. "I can do a lot more," she said, and licked her lips so there would be no mistaking what kind of pleasure she was referring to.

He laughed huskily and raised a brow. "Are you using me for sex?" he asked with feigned indignation.

She grinned up at him, feeling ridiculously happy. And hopeful. "Maybe."

He groaned. "I can't believe these words are leaving my mouth, but I didn't come over here in hopes of getting a blow job. I was actually hoping that tonight could be our first official date."

Another shock rippled through her, that he'd actually thought this evening through. "Our first date is pizza, ice cream, and a scary movie?"

The corner of his mouth quirked, and he rubbed a hand along the slight evening stubble on his jaw. "I'm not one to wine and dine. Hell, I don't even *like* wine, but if that's what you want, I'll take you anywhere you want to go."

Last night with Blake, Katrina had learned that she wasn't a wine-and-dine kind of woman, either. "What you brought over is absolutely perfect." And for them, it truly was.

"Then let's eat the pizza while it's still warm."

While she poured the root beer over ice, Mason served up the pizza, and they took their meal to her small dining table and sat next to each other. They talked about work for a while, their exchange effortless, easy, and familiar. And for the first time in a long while, Katrina felt happy. She was so glad to have her best friend back, because she'd missed this kind of casual, comfortable conversation with him. But she couldn't deny the zing of excitement inside her knowing he truly wanted something more.

He ate two pieces of pizza and went back for a third while she finished her second slice at a much slower pace. While she chewed a bite, Mason's expression changed to something more serious, and his brow creased as he seemed to contemplate something that was in his head.

"Everything okay?" she asked, wondering where his mind had gone and what he was thinking.

He set his crumpled napkin on his plate, pushed it aside, and turned his head to look at her. "You know, there's something I've been wanting to talk to you about since Vegas, but there really hasn't been a good time."

So much had happened during that weekend, and she had no idea where this chat was headed. "Okay."

"That last night when we were together . . . I felt those scars on your hip," he said, bringing up a topic she had no desire to discuss with him. Ever. "You didn't want to talk about it then, which I respected."

He stared at her gently but intently, and the pizza in her stomach suddenly felt as though it had turned to lead in the pit of her belly. A sense of dread welled up inside her, and she desperately tried not to let her panic show. He hadn't asked her a question *yet*, and she wasn't going to offer up details until she knew exactly what he wanted to know. Even then, she wasn't sure she could bear to tell him the truth.

He reached over, took her hand in his, and smoothed his thumb across her knuckles. "I know all about the cuts on your arm and why they happened," he said, reminding her of the day they'd met and how protective he'd been, even though he'd been a stranger at the time. "And I know you went to therapy after everything with your stepfather, to help you with controlling the urge to cut. You told me back then that it was over, that you wouldn't do it again . . . . In fact, you promised."

She swallowed the thick knot rising in her throat. She *had* made Mason that promise, and at the time, she'd meant her vow because she'd *believed* it. But then again, she'd never anticipated that a few years later, yet another set of devastating circumstances would send her spiraling back into such a dark, desolate place. She'd been so overcome with anger and emotional anguish that the only way to escape and cope with her humiliation and shame had been to turn all that mental suffering into the kind of physical pain that would guarantee to soothe and calm her bleak thoughts. If only for a little while.

He released a slow breath. "I need to know when those cuts happened," he said, drawing her out of his troubling thoughts. "Was it recently?"

His gaze was unwavering, his tone so full of concern and caring that Katrina wanted to cry and confess the whole terrible, awful truth that she'd never shared with anyone. But she didn't want him to look at her differently, to *see* her differently, so she settled for a vague, but truthful, response.

"No. It was back in high school." *Our senior year. Right before graduation.*

His fingers continued to stroke along her wrist where the butterfly tattoos on her arm began. "What happened to make you cut again?"

Your best guy friend at the time raped me, she thought, but the horrible words stuck in her throat. "I had a relapse." That much was honest.

"Why didn't you tell me?" he asked, the tenderness in his gaze nearly her undoing.

She glanced away from his too-intense stare, relieved he hadn't pushed her on the reasons behind her actions. "Because I was . . . ashamed."

His fingers touched her jaw until she looked at him again, and this time, he seemed troubled by her reply. "I'm your best friend, Katrina. You're supposed to share everything with me, and I hate that you went through something so painful by yourself. Even if it was back in high school. And now that I'm your . . . boyfriend," he said with a slight grin. "Okay, that was weird to say to a woman for the very first time in my life. But I don't ever want you to feel that you can't talk to me about anything. I'm always here for you. *Always.* Understood?"

She knew it wouldn't do any good to bring up what had happened all those years ago, except to expose her own insecurities and humiliation. Connor

Stevens had been out of their lives for eight years. After graduation, he'd gone into the military as a Marine, and as far as Katrina knew, Connor and Mason had lost touch, so there was no reason for her to rehash that part of her past. Cutting really and truly was behind her and had been for a long time.

"Promise me, Katrina," Mason said, his tone firm.

She nodded and pushed out a smile. "Yes, I promise," she said as she stood and started collecting their dirty dishes, desperate to move on from the conversation. "Now let's go watch our scary movie."

While she cleaned up the kitchen and put the leftover pizza in the refrigerator, Mason went into the living room and set up the movie. By the time she was done and joined him, the horror flick was ready to go. Her couch was wide with an ottoman they could push directly up against the sofa, which enabled them both to recline next to each other. She took the inside against the cushions, and after dimming the lights, Mason settled in beside her.

As the movie started, Katrina didn't hesitate to nestle up to his side, but she couldn't deny that this time felt different than the other friendlier times they'd cuddled together for a movie. He wrapped an arm around her so she could lay her head comfortably on his chest, and her legs were draped in between his. He played with her hair, running the strands through his fingers and occasionally skimming his thumb along the side of her neck, making her very aware of him and the slow, heated thrum of desire coursing through her.

DIRTY SEXY INKED

She loved snuggling with him as a girlfriend so much more because now she had full permission to slide her hand beneath his T-shirt and run her fingers over his tight abs. While he seemed focused on the movie, she casually stroked her hand along his toned stomach and up to his chest, then turned her head and placed a warm, damp kiss against his throat as her fingers grazed over a taut nipple.

Lightning quick, he grabbed her hand and turned his body toward hers, pinning her against the soft cushions, his body half on top of hers. He feigned a fierce frown as he looked down at her. "Dammit, this is our first date and I'm trying to be good."

She nipped at his jaw, and he groaned. "I like the bad Mason so much better."

He released her wrist and settled his hand on the curve of her waist beneath her camisole. "You're making it really *hard* to concentrate on the movie."

"I know." She laughed, happy to be back to their playful banter. "Wanna make out instead?"

His eyes dropped to her mouth, his gaze turning hungry. "Jesus, do you really think I'd say no to that?"

"I was hoping you wouldn't," she whispered as she tucked her fingers into the waistband of his jeans and pulled his hips to hers. The solid, tempting length of his erection nudged against her lower belly, and in response, her body softened even more. "And if you're really lucky, I might even let you get to fourth base," she teased.

The last thing she saw was his wicked grin before

he dropped his mouth over hers and she was lost in a sizzling, panty-melting kiss that quickly had her moving and rubbing restlessly against him. Minute by minute, the kisses grew hotter. Deeper. More demanding. His mouth claimed, his lips consumed, and the slide and swirl of his sinful tongue drove her wild for more.

The movie completely forgotten, she moaned restlessly and tugged on the top button of his jeans, wanting to feel him pulsing in her hand as she stroked his length. It felt like it had been forever since she'd touched him, had his shaft moving deep inside of her, and she ached to have him back where he belonged.

A deep, guttural growl tore from his throat as he lifted his mouth from hers. He stared down at her with an undeniable carnal heat glittering in his eyes. "I take it we're moving on to second base?"

She bit her swollen bottom lip, needing more than fondling through their clothes. She wanted them off so she could feel skin to skin. "I'd rather skip second base and get right to third," she said as she anxiously pushed his shirt up to his chest.

Helping her, he lifted up so he could pull the shirt the rest of the way over his head and dropped it to the floor behind him. "Just to be clear, what is your version of third base?"

She lifted her gaze to his and gave him a sultry, seductive smile. "Your mouth on my bare breasts and your hand between my legs," she said huskily. "I'm pretty sure orgasms are a requirement of making it past third base."

He chuckled lightly. "Duly noted. Take off your shorts and panties so there's nothing in my way of touching you."

Anticipation swirled inside of her, and she shoved both garments down her legs and kicked them off the couch so that she was naked from the waist down. As he shifted and moved a jean-clad knee between her legs, she pressed her palm to his warm, naked flesh as her arousal climbed a few more notches. God, he had a gorgeous body. Tattooed arms. Chiseled chest and abs. And a cock made for her pleasure. Yeah, she couldn't wait for that part.

Before she could slide her fingers back down to his waistband, Mason instead pushed her to her back and dragged the hem of her camisole up her torso. "Put your hands over your head so I can take this off," he ordered softly.

As directed, she raised her arms high as he pulled the top up and over her head. But instead of removing it completely, he twisted the thin shoulder straps and the rest of the material tight around her wrists so that they were bound together. With one hand, he pinned them on the couch above her head so that she was completely bared to him.

She felt equal measures of vulnerability and excitement. He soothed the former and fanned the flames of the latter as he slowly, deliberately trailed his gaze from her face, all the way down to her thighs. When he finally made his way back up to her eyes again, his features were etched with adoration and lust.

He pressed his face against her neck, his breath hot and damp against her skin as he licked a sizzling path all the way up to her ear. "I'm going to make you feel so fucking good."

She shivered, her breasts swelling as her breathing escalated. "I know. You always do," she said, and expressed her own desire. "But I want to touch you, too."

He shook his head, his dark, silky hair brushing against her bare shoulder as he bit her earlobe. "That's why I restrained your hands. So I can take full advantage of this soft, sweet body. So I'm in complete control of your pleasure. All you have to do is close your eyes and feel."

She already felt so much. Physically, yes, but emotionally, her heart was wide open and completely his. With one of the hands secured above her head, he entwined their fingers, the gesture so sensual and intimate it made her ache deep inside.

His free hand cupped her breast, his fingers squeezing and plucking at the stiff crest until her lips parted on a soft moan. His hot, wet mouth latched on to her other rock-hard nipple. His tongue swirled around the tip, his teeth adding a slight sting of pain as he lightly bit her flesh, making her whimper and her spine arch to push more of her breast between his lips. Seemingly knowing what she wanted, what she needed, he drew her deeper, the suctioning pull of his mouth so exquisite it made her wild.

And it made her beg. "Mason, *please*," she rasped. "I need your fingers *lower*."

He chuckled against her breast as his one hand skimmed down her quivering stomach. A single finger dipped inside of her navel, teasing and tormenting her. "Lower *here?*" he murmured, one hundred percent bad boy.

She opened her eyes and tried to glare at him, but the hot, dominant look on his face only made her realize that between her tied up hands and the knee wedged in between hers, she was completely at his mercy.

"Touch me . . . between my legs," she said breathlessly.

His fingers caressed along the inside of her thigh, bypassing her aching sex. "Here?" he asked, oh-so-innocently.

She was dying, and with every stroke of his fingers on her body, no matter where, it only amplified the pulsing need he was blatantly avoiding. "Mason . . . "

"Maybe you need to be more specific," he suggested with a devilish grin as he flicked his tongue across her nipple again. "Come on, Kitty-Kat. Talk dirty to me. Tell me in filthy detail what you want so I can give it to you."

Oh, God, oh, God, oh, God. The words were in her head, then in her mouth, and finally on the tip of her tongue. She spoke them before she lost the nerve. "Rub my clit with your fingers."

He rewarded her with a satisfied smile. "See, that

wasn't so hard, was it?" he asked as he *finally* stroked his fingers over and around that hard, sensitive nub.

She gasped as the bundle of nerves came alive beneath his skillful touch, and she closed her eyes and let her head fall back as he worked his magic. Her hips started to grind against his hand, and she felt so empty deep inside. This time, her dirty request came without hesitation.

"Fuck me with your fingers," she moaned shamelessly.

She gasped as he immediately filled her up with the thrust of two deft fingers, and her breath paused in her throat. He held them unmoving deep inside of her, along with the concentrated pressure of his thumb on her clit, leaving her suspended somewhere between frustration and sublime ecstasy.

His mouth came back to her ear, his voice dark and possessive. "You ready to come apart for me, baby?"

"*Yes*," she pleaded.

He exhaled a harsh breath and pumped his fingers in and out of her, hard and deep, while his thumb worked her clit in fast, relentless circles. So many sensations rocketed through her, and she tightened her fingers around the ones he'd laced with hers above her head, needing an anchor as her body shook from the force of her climax.

When her limbs stopped quaking and she finally came down from her high, she opened her eyes and found Mason looking at her, watching as she recovered. He'd released the camisole from around her wrists, and she slowly drew her arms back down. The hand that had just given her so much pleasure was now splayed on her stomach, but there was no mistaking the hard ridge of his erection beneath the fly of his jeans that was digging into her hip, reminding her that she was one step ahead of him in this game of *bases* they'd decided to play.

Smiling drowsily and uncaring that the scary moving was still playing in the background, she turned slightly to rub her body up against his like a satisfied cat. "You ready to score with a home run?" she asked as she skimmed her palms down his stomach, more than ready to go a second round, but this time with him buried inside her.

He stopped the hands traveling south and brought them back up to his chest. "Not tonight, Kitty-Kat."

She was stunned, shocked, and confused. "Why not?"

A chill passed over her bare skin, and when she shivered, he reached for the blanket she always left draped over the back of the couch and covered her with it, tucking her close to his side.

Then, he gently brushed a few strands of hair away from her cheek and tipped her face up to his so she was looking directly into his gorgeous blue eyes. "Don't doubt for a second that I want you, but I don't have a condom with me, and I won't risk having sex without using one. But most importantly, I didn't come over here for that tonight, though I can't deny I loved giving you that orgasm. It was fucking hot watching you come like that."

"Oh." Her mind was reeling from everything he'd just revealed. It said a lot about his true intentions that he hadn't come over prepared to have sex. And when she thought back, she'd been the one to initiate what had just happened.

His gaze turned serious. "I also want to tell you . . . despite my reputation, I've always gotten tested regularly, and the last time was right before Vegas. I'm clean."

"Thank you for telling me," she said, appreciating his honesty. It wasn't an easy conversation to have, but it was an important one. "And just for the record, as of a year ago and after my last relationship, I'm clean, as well."

He grinned playfully at her. "I'd say you were a bit of a *dirty* girl tonight, but in the best possible way," he said, reminding her of those filthy words she'd spoken, and how much they'd turned her on. "And I liked it. A lot."

"Me, too," she admitted, returning his smile. With him, she felt free to be that woman who embraced her sensuality, who could enjoy darker, more forbidden depths of sex. Because she trusted him and knew that it came from a place of pleasure, not degradation.

Not wanting to think about those *degrading* memories when they were part of a past she no longer wanted to relive, she curled her body into Mason's while he went back to watching the movie. She loved how safe and protected he made her feel, when no other man had ever come close to giving her that sense of security that she'd always craved.

And that was something she never wanted to lose.

Chapter Eleven

THREE WEEKS OF committed bliss had never felt so damn good, Mason thought as he cast a glance at Katrina while checking his inventory at his workstation. She was standing up at the front counter of the shop talking to Jasmine while pointing to something on the computer screen that they were both looking at. He took a moment to appreciate how gorgeous and sexy she looked today in her cherry-red pencil skirt, a white button-up blouse, and a pair of leopard-print heels that added a naughty element to the otherwise prim outfit.

So much had changed between them since that night when he'd gone over to her place with pizza, and not just the fact that Katrina was now his girlfriend. God, he *loved* how that sounded. Loved even more that their relationship was back to normal, except with smoking-hot sex whenever they wanted it. Which was often. He couldn't get enough of her, and didn't think he ever would, which was shocking considering he'd spent the past twelve years immersing himself in meaningless hookups in an attempt to escape a painful past. He'd avoided any kind of emotional involvement with a woman, because he'd always feared that the person he was with would eventually see how fucked-up he was and would leave.

But Katrina ... she'd been through everything with him, and not once had she wavered in her friendship. She knew all about his shitty past and hadn't run or cut him out of her life. She'd seen him through some of the worst times in his life, had endured his wild and rebellious behavior, and she was still here.

And now, she was his.

How was it that the one woman he'd refused to get involved with because of his fear of losing her was actually the one woman who made him feel whole and complete? Like she was his other half that he hadn't even known was missing until now. She made him feel calm and focused deep inside. Peaceful in a way that kept him centered and grounded, and she made him want to be a better man for *her*.

He'd always loved Katrina, but over the past few weeks, he'd fallen *in love* with her, and it was the single best feeling he'd ever experienced. The rush of emotions she evoked from him every single day was better than any other high he'd ever scored. As sappy as it sounded—and he'd never admit it to either of his brothers—being crazy in love was the best drug *ever*.

He was waiting for the perfect moment to tell her how he felt, and to suggest that she move into his place with him because that's where she belonged as far as he was concerned. In his bed. In his life. Every single day and night.

Needing a few supplies for his station, Mason went to the storeroom and gathered up a box of sterile gloves and grabbed more of the biohazard containers they used to dispose of used needles. He tucked a roll of paper towels under his arm, and just as he was leaving the back room, he heard Katrina's playful laughter, which prompted him to glance in her direction again to see what had amused her.

Not what, but who. Blake Cavanaugh.

The other man was standing up at the front counter, leaning casually toward Katrina, looking as charming and charismatic as always as he spoke to her, and there was nothing Mason could do to stop the shaft of jealousy that twisted in his stomach. He wasn't close enough to hear their conversation, but it didn't matter, because all he could think about was the fact that Katrina had dated the other guy—okay, one evening, but still a *date*—and it was obvious that Blake was still smitten with her.

Back off, fucker. She's mine, Mason thought possessively as he opened a drawer in his station and put his extra supplies inside. And each time Blake coaxed a laugh out of Katrina, that acid in Mason's stomach burned hotter, and the Neanderthal inside of him had to resist the urge to pound on his chest and make it clear that Katrina was *his* woman.

But instead of getting into a pissing match with Blake, Mason decided to handle the situation in a much more appropriate manner later. With Katrina. Thank God he was in between appointments, which gave him plenty of time to properly *punish* her.

Pulling his cell phone from his pocket, he typed in a text message and sent it to her. *Go to the restroom and take off your panties, then meet me in my office. Right now.*

Mason watched as Katrina picked up her phone, unlocked the screen, then read his note. Very slowly, she turned her head to look at him, her eyes wide and incredulous with her own silent message, *Are you kidding me?*

He smirked and tapped out another text. *Don't test me, baby, unless you'd prefer I come over there and toss you over my shoulder in front of God and Blake, and fucking take you there myself. DO IT NOW.*

Once she was done reading his second message, she glanced back at Blake and said something. The other man smiled and nodded, then headed over to Caleb's station for an appointment he must have had. Without looking at Mason, Katrina headed toward the hallway to the restroom, and he went to the office to wait for her.

A large wooden desk dominated the area, but the surface was neat and cleared off, which was Katrina's doing. She always kept everything orderly and put away, while he tended to leave loose paperwork all over the place. Right now, he truly appreciated her organizational tendencies, since it gave him a flat, uncluttered surface to fuck her on, or against, depending on how things played out.

The thought made his cock throb impatiently.

He opened the middle drawer and pulled out the wooden ruler inside just as Katrina slipped into the office—her face flushed with what Mason knew was the beginning glow of arousal—and shut the door behind her.

"Lock it," he ordered, as he caught a glimpse of the white silk fisted in one of her hands. "Then come here and give me your panties."

She secured the door, then walked toward him in those hot, fuck-me heels, her pretty eyes filled with excitement and curiosity, too. "Umm, why are you doing this?" she asked, her voice already husky with awareness and desire.

Everyone knew that he and Katrina were together as a couple, but they'd never—surprisingly—had sex anywhere in the shop. Looked like they were about to rectify that oversight, and benefit from the added thrill of doing it somewhere they could get caught. And Katrina certainly wasn't objecting. But then again, he'd discovered that she loved to role-play. Loved it even more when he got bossy and aggressive and took charge. *God, she was so fucking perfect.*

He put his hand out, and she automatically dropped the lacy thong into his palm, which he promptly shoved into the front pocket of his jeans. "You seriously have to ask that question?"

A naughty smile curved the corner of her mouth, making him even harder than he already was. "Does this have anything to do with me talking to Blake?" she asked oh-so-innocently.

Mason smacked the wooden ruler against his palm, and right before his eyes, her nipples tightened and pushed like twin pebbles against her blouse. Oh, yeah, she was already turned on. The uneven rise and fall of her chest and the way her tongue absently touched her bottom lip gave her away.

He narrowed his gaze, feigning displeasure. "You were laughing and smiling and flirting with him."

"He was flirting with *me*," she said, her voice breathless.

"And you *let* him, when you knew full well that I'd see." He circled around where she stood, until he was standing behind her, and smoothed his palm over the sweet curve of her ass and squeezed. "You need to be punished for being such a tease, and to remind you who you belong to. And because I'm feeling generous, I'm going to give you a choice for your punishment. The wooden ruler or my hand?"

She moaned softly and turned her head to look over her shoulder at him, her eyes glazed over with heated lust. "Mason . . . "

He grabbed a handful of her silky hair and pulled her head farther back, until his mouth was against her ear. "Choose, or I'll decide for you," he demanded sharply, and snapped the wooden stick against her thigh.

She jumped from the unexpected smack as a squeak of surprise escaped her throat. "Your hand," she replied quickly.

Releasing her hair, he moved back in front of her and put the ruler aside since he wouldn't be needing it. "Pull your skirt up, all the way to your waist. Show me what belongs to me."

She started inching up the hem, her gaze heavy-lidded as she revealed her smooth, bare thighs and neatly trimmed pussy, the delicate folds in between those gorgeous legs already plump and glistening with moisture. He inhaled a deep breath. *Fuck*, he could smell how aroused she was, and the blood in his veins thickened with a sharp, unrelenting hunger.

Holding her gaze, he slowly dragged his fingers up the inside of her thigh, until they sank into the softest, wettest, most decadent heat he'd ever encountered. "Who is all this wetness for?"

"You," she said, her legs quivering as he delved even deeper, drawing more slick moisture from her body. "Only you."

"Don't ever forget that," he replied gruffly, enjoying the way she surrendered so beautifully for him. He caught her clit between two of his fingers and tugged gently, but firmly enough to make her moan softly. "This is mine. *You're* mine."

Her pretty green eyes dilated with a heat and hunger that matched his own. "Yes."

He dragged those same fingers slowly through that bit of heaven that was all his, and while she watched, he brought his hand up to his lips and sucked the alluring taste of her into his mouth.

"You are so goddamn sweet," he murmured, licking his fingers clean. "Like fucking candy. If you didn't need to be disciplined, I'd already be on my knees with my face and tongue buried in your pussy."

She started to pant, her expression etched with the same lust that was burning him up inside. He wanted to tear open her blouse and ravage her breasts, suck those tasty nipples into his mouth until she screamed, but she had to leave the office after this tryst, and that meant keeping her clothes intact while he defiled her in more pleasurable ways.

"Turn around and bend over with your arms on the desk," he commanded in a sharp tone. "I want your ass in the air for your punishment."

She didn't hesitate to comply, so eager to please knowing it would ultimately lead to her absolute pleasure. It always did. The fact that she made herself so vulnerable to him, that she trusted him to give her that satisfaction while he controlled how and when, was like a precious gift to him. And one he'd never take for granted. No, this dirty, sexy play was mutual, and shockingly, it brought him intimately closer to her every single time.

Mason stroked his palm over her bare bottom, taking a moment to appreciate the curve of her ass before he lifted his hand and smacked her, firmly enough that her flesh gave a little shake. Her back arched and she gasped at the stinging impact.

"That's for giving any other man that beautiful smile and sweet laugh that belongs to me." He swatted the other side, his dick pulsing at the sight of his large handprint appearing in a light shade of pink on her pale skin, marking her as his. "And that's for making me jealous."

She whimpered and shifted on her high heels, rubbing her thighs together to undoubtedly ease the ache in between. "Mason, please . . . " she begged softly.

Done teasing them both, he tore open the front of his jeans and shoved his pants and briefs down to his thighs, freeing his erection. "Spread your legs nice and wide for me, Kitty-Kat," he ordered, and while she braced her feet apart to make room for him in between, he took care of a condom.

Guiding the tip of his cock along her wet crevice, he found her opening and pushed the head inside just a few inches. A needy sound escaped her, and she shamelessly rocked back against him, seeking more of his length.

Giving them what they both desperately needed, he grasped her hips and slammed into her in one driving thrust, burying his shaft balls deep inside of her. She swallowed back a cry as he filled her, and he groaned at the way her body tightened around his cock as he tunneled in and out of her.

She suddenly pushed up on her hands, which angled her back and thrust her hips out farther, made him delve deeper with every undulating grind against her ass. "Mason," she panted wildly. "I'm going to come so hard . . . I'm going to scream," she said as her voice rose in volume, along with the orgasm he could feel fluttering around his cock.

Jesus. If they were at his place, he wouldn't give a shit if she shouted her throat raw—hell, he'd fucking love it. But they were in his office with employees and clients a few yards away, and he wasn't about to let anyone else hear her cries of passion. They belonged to him, just as she did, and he didn't share.

Before she could let loose those wails, he reached up and wrapped his fingers gently around her neck, then slid his hand up until he was gripping her jaw and turned her face to the side. His mouth was there, waiting for hers, and he crushed their lips together just in time to muffle any loud noises she would have made. His tongue tangled with hers, her body clenching around his shaft as she came and he continued to plunge into her from behind—fast and hard and deep.

God, he wasn't going to last long, either. She was so hot, so uninhibited, and he was suddenly overwhelmed by the depth of his feelings for her, that he could want and need and love someone as much as he did Katrina. So openly and completely. She owned his heart. She was the other half of his soul. And he never wanted to live his life without her in it.

The thought sent a heated rush of adrenaline surging through him, triggering an orgasm that was so intense that he was grateful that Katrina's mouth stifled his own hoarse shouts that would have reverberated off the walls if he hadn't still been kissing her.

It took them both a little while to recover, but eventually he moved away from her to take care of the condom. She turned around to face him as she pushed down the hem of her skirt so it was properly back in place, but there was no denying the pink afterglow of bliss shading her complexion, or the gleam in her eyes that expressed pure sexual satisfaction.

The words *I love you* nearly came tumbling out of Mason's mouth at that moment, but he caught them just in time. As badly as he wanted to share that declaration, he didn't want it to happen in his office after a round of possessive sex, no matter how good it had been for both of them. He wanted them to be alone and him completely focused on Katrina when he revealed his feelings for the first time. He wanted the moment to be special and memorable. She deserved that.

She tucked in her blouse where it had come loose, a sexy smile on her lips. "If I'm going to get in trouble like this every time I smile at another man, it might happen more often."

"You're a goddamn tease," he said, grinning back at her.

She didn't deny it. "Can I have my panties back, please?"

"No." Her mouth dropped open, and it took effort for him not to laugh. "Consider it part of your punishment, baby." He hooked his fingers into the waistband of her skirt, pulled her to him, and brushed his mouth against hers. "I want you to feel those handprints on your ass every time your skirt brushes against your bottom, or you sit down, and without any panties on for the rest of the day, you'll be sure to remember who you belong to, and that you're *mine*."

He'd been just about to kiss her again when someone knocked on the door. Startled by the interruption, Katrina jumped back, her eyes wide and her face coloring with embarrassment at the realization of how close they'd been to getting caught.

"Mason?" Jasmine called from the other side of the door, and turned the knob, only to find it wouldn't open.

"Yes?" he responded casually, while Katrina looked mortified, because there was only one reason they'd lock the door with both of them inside the office.

"There's someone here to see you," the other girl said.

"I'll be right out." Mason had about a half hour before his next appointment, so he assumed it was a product vendor, which happened all the time.

He waited a solid minute to make sure Jasmine was gone before he spoke to Katrina again. "Are you okay?" For as much as he'd enjoyed what had just happened, he wanted to make sure *she* was fine before he left.

She arched a sassy brow. "Why, do I look like I've just been screwed?"

Screwed was a word he would have used in the past to describe a meaningless fling, but right now, in this moment with Katrina, it wasn't a connotation he wanted related to her at all. "No, you look absolutely beautiful," he said, and meant it. He'd given her that flush on her face, that dreamy look in her eyes, and he was damned proud of it.

"I'll leave first and you can come out whenever you're ready," he said, and gave her a quick kiss on her lips before heading out of the office.

Chapter Twelve

NEEDING TIME TO gather her emotions and her composure, Katrina sat down in the leather chair behind Mason's desk. She honestly didn't care who suspected that they'd just indulged in a little afternoon quickie, but she appreciated that Mason cared enough to make sure that she was okay.

So much had changed between the two of them in the three weeks since they'd returned from Vegas. They'd gone from best friends to lovers to something that was beginning to feel a lot more intimate and permanent. She finally felt like she was in a really good place with Mason, and she couldn't be happier—even if there was a tiny part of her that was still guarded about their relationship.

It wasn't as though Mason had done anything to make her feel insecure. No, it was her own stupid doubts and uncertainties that kept rearing their ugly head with questions she had no answers for. Like, *would Mason get tired of her and realize he preferred being single because that's all he'd ever known and she'd be left with a shattered heart? Or, was he ready for something more committed, like marriage, and then a family, or was that not even on his radar?* And most importantly, *was he capable of loving her as more than just an intimate friend?*

She'd like to believe that was possible, that in time he'd realize she was a woman he could spend his life with. She didn't doubt his sincerity in this relationship, and she knew that he cared deeply for her, but there were always those fears that kept her cautious with her heart, when she wanted so badly to tell him how she felt—that she'd loved him for years. Unsure of where *he* was emotionally, she wasn't prepared to take that risk. Nor did she want to put him on the spot and force him to say something he wasn't ready to admit or say back.

So, for now, she was trying to just enjoy the excitement of having Mason's attention, of knowing that *she* was the woman he brought home every night and slept with. Even though she'd been in love with him for so long, she had to take into consideration that this whole relationship thing was new for Mason, and she needed to give everything time. She'd already seen a huge change in him in the past two weeks, and as much as she appreciated Blake Cavanaugh's job offer, she'd given him a call and declined the position. He'd been disappointed, but let her know that if she ever changed her mind, the job offer would still stand.

Right now, she was content. Her issues about working at Inked, and looking for another job, had never been about wanting something more, but rather had been a result of her inner conflict with Mason and how difficult it had become to work around him day after day. But that was no longer a problem, and she wasn't going anywhere anytime soon.

Figuring that enough time had passed that she could slip out of the office without all eyes on her, she headed back into the main area of the shop, all too aware of the fact that she had no panties on, and that they were still in Mason's pocket. He was so bad, in the very best way, and she couldn't deny that she liked him knowing and thinking about her being completely bare beneath the skirt. By the time they got to his place tonight, he'd undoubtedly be hot and bothered and would probably pin her against the nearest wall the moment they walked into his house.

She shivered at the delightful, sexy thought as she glanced over at Mason's station. He was talking to a big, buff-looking guy with broad shoulders, tattooed arms, and sandy-blond hair that was cropped close along the sides—she couldn't see the man's face since he was turned away from her—but the happy, expressive look on Mason's face and the occasional laugh she heard told Katrina that it was someone he knew.

Before Katrina reached the front counter to talk to Jasmine, Mason called out to get her attention. "Katrina, come on over here," he said enthusiastically. "You'll never guess who's back in town."

Curious to know who the person was that Mason was so excited about, she started toward his station. As she stepped into the cubicle, the man turned around, and when Katrina looked up at his face, she came to an abrupt, apprehensive stop a few feet away from him.

Everything inside of her flashed hot, then ice seemed to run through her veins as she met Connor Stevens's cool gray eyes. The man who'd been one of Mason's friends in high school. The guy who'd sexually assaulted her right before graduation, without remorse or guilt or an ounce of regret. No, instead, he'd called her a whore and a tramp, had told her *she'd asked for it*, then threatened her so she'd never tell a soul what had happened.

And she hadn't. But now, after eight years of being gone, he was back, and she had to forcibly swallow the sick feeling rising in her throat as all those horrific memories came flooding back as she stared at him. He no longer looked like a teenage boy. After being in the military for years, he was built and muscular and, to her, intimidating in size, and the very thought made her feel as though she suddenly couldn't breathe.

He gave her a friendly smile, and there was no trace of the cocky, younger version of Connor who'd been more of a delinquent than Mason had been. "Hey, Katrina," he said amicably. "It's great to see you again."

She was so paralyzed by anxiety that she couldn't speak or move, even when Connor closed the distance between them and hugged her as if nothing had ever happened. She flinched away from him and didn't return the friendly embrace—she could barely stand to have him touch her without her having a full-blown panic attack. After a moment, he pulled away and stepped back, and if he'd noticed how stiff and unresponsive she'd been, his expression didn't show it.

"Isn't it great seeing Connor again?" Mason asked her, oblivious to the turmoil roiling inside of her. And why wouldn't he be? Mason had no clue what his *friend* had done.

Katrina's head swam and she felt light-headed. She couldn't bring herself to answer Mason and say something that wasn't true. All she knew was that she had to get away from Connor before her legs gave out on her and she either passed out or threw up. Hell, both were a very real possibility.

"I need to make a phone call to a client about a commissioned drawing," she lied as she backed away.

"No problem," Connor said easily as he leaned against the counter in Mason's station and crossed his arms casually over his solid chest. "I'm sure I'll see you around."

Katrina managed, just barely, to suppress a full-body shudder. She hated the way that sounded, because she didn't ever want to *see* him again, yet here he was. And for how long?

"Yeah, we'll all have to get together again, like old times," Mason suggested, clearly looking forward to hanging out with his old friend again.

Trying desperately to maintain her composure—because she refused to let Connor think he affected her in any way—Katrina walked back to the office while Mason and Connor resumed their conversation. She closed the door and sat back down on the chair behind the desk and took deep breaths to calm the anxiety trying to claw its way to the surface. Along with the shame and humiliation she'd thought she'd left behind. Obviously not.

Her stomach was in knots, and she couldn't stop the awful memories of that night with Connor as they played in her mind like a horror movie. Fifteen minutes ago, she'd sat in this same chair and felt hopeful about her future. Now, she was filled with dread, because if this grown-up Connor was anything like the teenage boy he'd been, he had the ability to ruin her, and the power to destroy the fragile relationship she'd just begun with Mason.

She rubbed her sweaty palms down her skirt, trying to give the situation a positive spin, as she'd been taught to do by her therapist all those years ago. Katrina believed that people had the ability to change their behavior or actions if they truly wanted to—Mason was proof of that. Maybe after spending so many years in the military, Connor was now a changed man from the belligerent, hostile, arrogant kid he'd been. Maybe with all that rigid discipline, he'd become a better person.

It was a possibility, and Katrina hoped it was true. But unless Connor acknowledged what had happened between them, and apologized for what he'd done and she believed he was sincerely regretful, then there was absolutely no way she could be anywhere near him. The fear and anxiety inside of her was too real, and right now, she didn't trust him any more than she had back in high school.

Once Katrina felt like she was back in control of her emotions, she retrieved the laptop she used for payroll and accounting and turned it on to get some work done in the safety of the office—where no one would bother her and she wouldn't have to overhear or watch the bromance between Connor and Mason.

About an hour later, Mason walked into the office, his eyes bright and his expression cheerful. He sat down in one of the chairs in front of the desk, clearly wanting to talk.

"Wasn't it great seeing Connor again?" Mason asked, but thankfully didn't wait for her answer, because obviously *he* was excited about seeing his old friend. "I can't believe how long it's been and now he's back in town."

"For how long?" Katrina asked, praying that it was a temporary stop for Connor and he'd be moving on soon.

"He was discharged from the military a few months ago and decided to move back to Chicago," Mason said, and Katrina felt that pressure in her chest return. "He's working at a friend's motorcycle shop until he finds something more permanent, but as far as I know, he's staying in the area."

CARLY PHILLIPS & ERIKA WILDE

Katrina knew that Connor didn't have any family, so yeah, he was probably getting in touch with old friends now that he was a civilian again. He'd been raised in foster homes most of his life, and the last she'd heard, right before he'd left for the Marines, was that the family he'd been with had been relieved to see him go because he'd been so much trouble. According to Mason at the time, Connor had gone into the service because it was either join the military and get a steady paycheck, or become homeless, since at eighteen he was an adult and no longer a ward of the state.

"He asked if I wanted to go hang out at Kincaid's with him tonight," Mason said. "Want to go with?"

She immediately shook her head. While she hated that Mason would be spending even more time with Connor, she wasn't about to be one of those girlfriends who didn't let her man have time with his guy friends. Nor did she want to explain her own aversion to being around Connor, because if Mason ever confronted him with the truth, Katrina already knew what Connor's twisted version of events would be. And her biggest fear was that Mason would look at her differently, and treat her differently. Or worse, he'd believe Connor's lies as her mother had believed her stepfather's. And that would ultimately destroy her.

No, it was better all the way around if she just avoided anything that had to do with Connor, including hanging out with him in any way, shape, or form.

"I think I'll pass," she said as nicely as possible so Mason wouldn't question her decision. "I have some errands I want to do after work and some things I need to get done at the apartment, so you go ahead."

He tipped his head to the side, his eyes warm and caring. "I'll see you later tonight, then? I'll come over to your place afterward."

She nodded. "Sure. That sounds good."

But later that evening, the more Katrina thought about Mason spending time with Connor, then coming over and *talking* to her about Connor, she knew she wouldn't be able to handle any part of that conversation.

So, instead she sent Mason a text. *I have a headache and I'm going to bed early. I'll see you in the morning.*

A few minutes later, he replied. *Are you sure? Do you need me to bring you anything? I can leave right now and be there in a few minutes.*

Her throat closed up with a wave of emotion at how thoughtful Mason was being, that he was willing to leave the bar to be with her—she only had to say the words. But honestly, after the day she'd had, she just wanted to be alone tonight. *I'm good. I promise.*

It was a total lie. She was a wreck inside, and with Connor back, dredging up old memories, making them feel like current ones, she didn't know how she'd ever be okay again.

✧   ✧   ✧

MASON HAD NO idea what was going on with Katrina, but their relationship had gone from an amazing high to an all-time low in a matter of days. From her spending every night at his house to her making excuses that she had things to do, she was tired, or she wasn't feeling well and she wanted to sleep in her own bed.

The first few days, it was no big deal. But now it was Friday, the start of the weekend, and while he'd normally be doing something with Katrina, instead he was sitting at Kincaid's nursing a beer and waiting for Connor to join him for a drink because she'd blown him off with the pretense that she needed to work on a commissioned design for a client. That might be true, but the fact that she'd insisted on staying home alone to do it was the frustrating part for Mason.

He could feel her withdrawing from him both emotionally and physically, isolating herself, and he was at a complete loss as to why. When he asked, she always assured him she was *fine*, but he'd been Katrina's best friend long enough to know that she wasn't being honest. Even the times he'd tried to give her a spontaneous hug or kiss, she'd stiffen against him. The whole situation was scaring the shit out of Mason because he didn't know what was wrong, or what he'd done to make her so distant.

All he did know for certain was that something had to give, and soon.

"You ready to raise some hell tonight?" Connor asked as he finally arrived at Kincaid's and slid onto a barstool next to Mason's. He rubbed his hands together in anticipation. "Just like old times?"

Mason glanced at the other man, welcoming the distraction from his troubling thoughts of Katrina, and forced a grin. "I haven't raised hell in years." At least not like they had back in high school, when his teenage behavior had been fueled by anger, and his only goal had been to be as reckless and defiant as possible—just to piss off Clay, his teachers, and anyone else with authority.

"I think my wild days are pretty much behind me," Mason added, and it honestly felt good to be in a stable place in his life to say that and believe it. Without a doubt, he knew Katrina had a huge part in taming that wild and careless man he'd been.

"Naw, I think I could coax it back out of you," Connor said confidently, and waved Tara over, even though she was crazy busy with the Friday evening crowd.

When she arrived, Connor ordered two shots of cheap-grade tequila and downed both drinks as soon as Tara put the two glasses in front of him. "Getting wasted is a good start to the night," he said with a smirk, and glanced around at all the customers in the place.

The tables were filled up, as was the dance floor. People were having a good time, and suddenly Mason wanted to be anywhere else, but he didn't want to ditch his friend so soon after he'd arrived. It really was great seeing Connor again, and there was no doubt that the military had somewhat straightened him out. But over the past few days of Connor spontaneously stopping by the shop and meeting him at Kincaid's after work to reestablish their friendship, Mason was aware that he was still arrogant and cocksure, and even a bit of a hothead.

Just last night, some guy at the bar had accidentally bumped into Connor, and it was like a switch had been flipped, and he didn't hesitate to shove the other kid so hard that he'd landed on his ass. Even when the other guy had tried to apologize, Connor had gotten all up in his face, and Mason had had to step between them before he'd pummeled the customer for no good reason.

So, yeah, there were still traces of that volatile kid Connor had been. Mason would have thought that the military would have taught him how to curb those angry outbursts. And that's exactly what they were—sudden explosive impulses that seemed to come out of nowhere, and then in the next moment, he was fine again.

A part of Mason felt bad for Connor, because he knew that the guy had no family, and he was trying to renew old friendships so he had people to hang out with. And from the few stories that Connor had shared with him about being in Iraq, there was no denying that he'd been through hell and was hopefully just trying to find his footing again, and those anger issues would lessen in time.

"So, I know someone who can get us into an underground fight club," Connor said, bringing Mason's attention back to his friend again. "You interested in going tonight and placing some bets?"

As a teenager, Mason would have totally been on board. Hell, he probably would have been the one to suggest the idea. Now? The thought of watching gratuitous violence held no appeal to him. "I'll pass," he said with a shake of his head. "It's really not my thing."

"We could always go score some blow," Connor continued as he caught Tara's attention again and indicated he wanted two more shots of the same tequila. "What's a Friday night without a little nose candy?"

It had been years since Mason had touched the stuff. He had a good life now, a reputable business, and there was no way he'd jeopardize any of that for a quick high. "I'm not into that shit anymore."

"Jesus fucking Christ," Connor said, an edge of irritation in his voice that he washed down with both shots of liquor, one right after the other. "When did you get so damn boring? Is pussy still your thing? Because there's a helluva lot of it right in front of both of us, and I wouldn't mind taking advantage," he said, indicating the women in the bar who would be easy conquests.

"Yeah, it's still my thing," Mason finally snapped back with a glare while trying hard to tamp down his annoyance at Connor's persistence. "But I'm not interested in anyone but Katrina. I told you that she and I are seeing one another." And despite whatever she was going through right now, his feelings for her weren't going to change.

"She'll never have to know," Connor said with a careless shrug, his eyes a bit glassy as he grinned at Mason. "I won't say a thing."

"Not interested," Mason said again, this time more succinctly.

"I get it," Connor said after a moment, a smirk curving his lips. "Gotta say, she's a hot piece of ass."

Mason's entire body tensed at Connor's crude, disrespectful comment, and his hand balled into a tight fist on the surface of the bar. "Excuse me?" he said with more calm than he was feeling inside. The guy was damn lucky that Mason hadn't clocked him in the face for his crass remark.

As if realizing he might have gone too far, Connor held up his hands in an attempt to diffuse the situation. "Jesus, that was a compliment. Relax, dude."

"I don't give a shit if it was a compliment," Mason replied heatedly, and he also didn't care if it was the alcohol in Connor's system that was responsible for his unfiltered statement. "Don't fucking talk about Katrina like that. *Ever.*"

There was a smug look in Connor's gaze that unsettled Mason for a moment, and then it was gone. "I gotta piss," the other man finally said to break up the tension swirling between them, then slid off the barstool and headed toward the restrooms.

Mason was grateful for the reprieve. He exhaled a harsh breath and scrubbed a hand down his face, knowing that the entire situation with Katrina had him

DIRTY SEXY INKED

on edge, which didn't help his disposition with Connor tonight. And until *they* were resolved as a couple,
he was going to be a gutted mess inside.

It took every ounce of willpower he possessed not
to head over to her place tonight and confront her,
because he'd learned over the years that Katrina was
the kind of person who internalized things for a while.
Sometimes longer than he was even aware of. And he
was honestly afraid that if he pushed her too hard, too
fast, too soon, she'd withdraw even further, to the
point that it would do irreparable damage to their new
and fragile relationship.

The thought of losing her, in any way, struck at the
heart of his fears and insecurities, which made it
difficult for him to give her the space that she seemed
to need right now. As much as it killed him, he'd allow
her the rest of the weekend alone, to hopefully come
to the conclusion to trust him with whatever issue was
driving this goddamn wedge between them.

But come Monday, they were going to talk and
hash out the problem, whether she wanted to or not.

Chapter Thirteen

KATRINA STARED AT the sharp butcher's knife in her hand, her heart beating hard and fast in her chest. It was late Sunday night, and one minute, she was slicing an apple to eat because she hadn't had anything of substance in her stomach all day, and the next second, the shiny steel blade was whispering to that weak part of her subconscious, promising her relief from the intense, emotional misery twisting inside her if only she'd press the sharp edge of the knife to her skin and slice it open.

She'd done it before, and she knew what to expect.

One cut, and all the horrible feelings would fade away as she embraced the physical rush of pain. Two slices, and she'd escape this awful reality she'd been living for the past week. Three deep lacerations, and she'd forget that Connor, a man who'd raped her so brutally, was insinuating himself back into Mason's life and pushing her out of it. Four slashes through her flesh, and she'd finally have the reprieve she desperately needed from the fear and anxiety that she now lived with on a daily basis.

A sob caught in her throat and hot, scalding tears filled her eyes. *What the hell am I doing?* Katrina immediately dropped the knife to the cutting board, refusing to revert to that terrible addiction that she knew would only offer a temporary release to the internal pain and increasing depression that was suffocating her. But mostly, she refused to let Connor's presence break her down even more emotionally. She refused to let him *win* and send her spiraling back into the depths of despair, where she'd spent the entire weekend. No amount of cutting and self-harm would change the situation or make Connor go away. And that meant she had to figure out a healthier way to deal with the situation and her anxiety.

Stepping away from the counter, she drew in a shaky breath and swiped away the tears on her cheeks, grateful for her own mental breakdown that was forcing her to make difficult decisions and take charge of her life again, instead of living in constant fear. Just as she'd taken control after her stepfather's abuse, and again after Connor's attack back in high school. She refused to allow such an asshole to have so much power over her emotions, and she would *not* let him come between her and Mason and destroy the one thing that made her so completely happy.

Which meant she had to tell Mason the truth, because if she couldn't be open and honest with him about *everything*, and trust him with something so dark and painful, then what hope did they have of a successful future? What hope did *she* have?

Decision made, she went into the living room, picked up her cell phone, and sent Mason a brief text. *I need to talk to you tomorrow.*

Seconds later, he replied. *I want to talk to you, too. But there's something important I have to do in the morning, and I won't be in the shop until around one.*

She couldn't help but wonder what was so important that he'd blocked off half of a Monday to do, but didn't ask. Considering that she'd shut him out for the past three days, she was grateful for whatever time he would give her. *That's fine. I'll see you then.*

BY TWELVE FORTY-FIVE the following afternoon, Katrina couldn't deny that her nerves were starting to get the best of her as she thought about her upcoming conversation with Mason, which, according to the clock on the wall at Inked, would be very soon.

She was sitting at the drafting table sketching an intricate design of a fairy for a woman's upper back, which gave her something to focus on instead of all the possible scenarios looping through her mind featuring Mason's various reactions to their discussion. She had no idea how everything was going to play out, but it didn't matter, because it wouldn't change the fact that she was finally going to confide in her best friend. Something she should have done back in high school after Connor had raped her.

She absently glanced up at the clock again. Not even five minutes had passed. So far, it had been a slow and mostly quiet morning, which was normal for a Monday. Derek and Caleb had had a few standing appointments, which they'd both finished by noon. With time free before their next customers, they'd decided to go out and grab a bite to eat for lunch. That left Katrina and Jasmine in the shop.

All morning long, Katrina had found herself wondering where Mason might be, and the only thing she could come up with was that he'd had some kind of plans with Connor. Last week, every day Connor had stopped by Inked in his attempt to reestablish his friendship with Mason and insinuate himself back into Mason's life. And every time he'd come into the shop, he'd tried to strike up a conversation with her, as if *they* were long-lost buddies. She'd kept her replies curt, and found it best if she just walked away so she didn't have to be in his presence or deal with the dread and unease that always accompanied his visits.

The front door to the shop opened, and knowing it was Mason, Katrina immediately glanced up—and felt as though she'd been kicked in the stomach as she watched Connor stroll in. By himself. She kept waiting for Mason to appear, to walk in behind him . . . but it never happened.

"Hey, Jasmine," Connor said, greeting the other

girl with a smile as he leaned against the front counter. "Is Mason here?"

Katrina didn't look in his direction—it was rude of her, but she didn't care—though she could see Connor in her peripheral vision as she sketched. The fact that he was asking for Mason meant they hadn't spent the morning together. *So where was he?*

"No, he's been out all morning," Jasmine replied in the same friendly manner she treated all people who came into the shop. "I'm not sure when he'll be back."

"Okay," Connor said easily. "Will you leave a message for him that I stopped by?"

"Sure thing."

Good, now he'll leave. Katrina exhaled a deep, calming breath and kept her head down, but as soon as she saw him coming toward the drafting table, her entire body tensed. She couldn't even move the pencil in her hand.

"Hey, Katrina," he said, stopping beside the table less than an arm's length away and invading way too much of her personal space.

The knot in her stomach tightened. "Hey," she muttered, because the last thing she wanted to do was antagonize him in any way. That was definitely one thing she remembered about him back in high school—he'd always had a short fuse. He might have outgrown it, but she wasn't taking any chances.

"You weren't around Saturday or Sunday," he said, and Katrina hated that he knew her schedule or had noticed her absence from the shop. "Big plans this past weekend?"

She couldn't do this. She couldn't just sit there and have any kind of conversation with him and pretend as though everything was fine and he'd never violated her in the worst way possible. Her heart was pumping so hard in her chest that it hurt, and she knew she had to get away from him. *Now.*

Without replying, she picked up a file folder from the drafting table that she'd set there earlier and moved off her chair in the opposite direction of where Connor stood, so there was no chance of her body touching his as she passed by.

Ignoring him completely, she walked on unsteady legs toward the back of the shop. "Jasmine, I'll be in the storeroom doing the inventory."

"Okay," the other girl replied, oblivious to any tension between Katrina and Connor.

As Katrina stepped into the back room, she heard Connor say, "I'll see you later, Jasmine," in a terse tone that was no doubt meant for *her.*

"Bye, Connor," Jasmine said, and the shop went quiet again.

Katrina set the file folder on a shelf and leaned against the wall, needing a few minutes alone to calm herself. Her palms felt clammy, and she was trembling as if it were forty degrees in the shop.

"Hey, Katrina," Jasmine called out. "Since it's quiet right now, I'm going to run down to the corner deli and get myself a sandwich for lunch. Do you want anything?"

"No," she said as loud as her hoarse, scratchy

voice would allow.

"I'll be back in fifteen minutes," Jasmine said, and once again, everything fell silent.

Katrina let her head drop back against the wall, closed her eyes, and drew deep, even breaths to ease the panicky sensation coursing through her. She'd barely calmed down when she heard the faint sound of footsteps that grew louder as they approached the back of the shop.

Mason was there. Finally!

Relief flooded her entire body, and she pushed away from the wall and started for the storeroom door . . . and came to an abrupt, sickening halt when Connor's big, solid frame blocked her path instead.

There was no holding back the gasp that ripped from her throat, and because he was imposing in size, she instinctively took a few steps back. Animosity glittered in his dark eyes as he followed her slowly but purposefully, until he had her cornered against the wall. There was no way to move around him without Connor easily grabbing her, *restraining her just as he had that long ago night.*

When a sneer curled the corner of his mouth, it reminded her of the bully he'd been. That mean look on his face also solidified that he *hadn't* changed, and he wasn't here to apologize or make amends for the past. Belligerent men like him, like her stepfather, didn't feel remorse for their actions. No, they believed they were entitled, especially when they weren't held accountable for their cruel and disgusting behavior.

Despite the apprehension surging through her, she lifted her chin, refusing to let him see any weakness that he could prey upon, even if she did feel incredibly vulnerable. "You need to leave, Connor," she said in a firm, strong voice. "Now."

He didn't move. Instead, his insolent gaze raked down the length of her, taking in the pretty vintage pinup style dress she'd chosen with such care today for *Mason*. She shuddered as Connor's lewd perusal lingered at the bodice and on her breasts before rising once again.

"Why are you being such a stuck-up bitch?" he asked as a muscle in his cheek ticked with barely suppressed anger. "Every time I come in here, you're rude and you blow me off. And you act like you're too good to even talk to me. What the fuck is your problem?"

She should have been afraid, considering there was no escape, they were alone, and he was physically stronger and had no issues using force with a woman, as she well knew. But all the rage and pain she'd buried for so many years found their way to the surface, and she embraced the strength and fortitude it gave her to confront him about that night.

"*You're* my problem, Connor," she said, shocked at her bravery, but she didn't stop there. "How can you come back here and expect everything to be just fine after what you did to me?"

Katrina hated the unapologetic smirk that he gave her, which he followed up with a callous laugh. "Are you still mad about that night before we graduated?" he asked in a mocking tone. "We were just having fun and things got a little rough. It wasn't a big deal."

"It wasn't fun, asshole," she yelled at him, and had to curl her hands into fists at her sides so she didn't claw his eyes out. "You pushed me into an empty room at that party. You pinned me down when I tried to get away. You put your hand over my mouth when I screamed. And then *you raped me*!" God, she'd had terrifying nightmares for months afterward, and every time she'd woken up in a panic, she'd felt as though she were reliving that horrifying attack all over again.

He braced a hand on the wall by her head and leaned closer. "Well, maybe if you weren't such a cock tease back then, it wouldn't have happened," he said, as if it had been her fault. "That short skirt you were wearing that night made you look like a tramp and begged a guy to fuck you, so I only did what you were asking for. Hell, you're a fucking tease even now and no better than you were back then."

"What a woman wears doesn't define whether you can screw her or not, you prick," she said, welcoming the surge of adrenaline that was pumping liquid courage through her veins, giving her the confidence to purge everything she'd kept bottled up for the past eight years. "I never teased you. I always hated you and did my best to keep my distance. You might have been able to convince Mason to be your friend in high school, but I never trusted you. And there was a reason why. You proved every one of my instincts correct that night when you assaulted me. You're nothing but a sorry excuse for a man."

His eyes blazed with malice. "And you're nothing but a fucking whore."

Without thinking, she slapped him across the face. So hard, it made his head snap to the side. He let out a heartless laugh, and when he looked at her again, his expression was ruthless enough to cause a frisson of real fear to trickle down her spine.

"See? You do like it rough, don't you?" he said in a low, taunting voice.

Before she could gauge his actions, he shoved her up against the wall so hard that the impact stole her breath. Trapping her there with his muscular body, he groped at one of her breasts and twisted his fingers into her hair with his other hand to force her head back right before he tried to kiss her.

This time, she wasn't going down without a fight.

She struggled against him, and the moment his mouth touched hers, she did the only thing she could and bit his lip as hard as she could, until she broke the skin and drew blood.

He jerked back with a howl, his expression furious. "Goddamn bitch," he ground out, and lifted a fist to punch her in the face.

Unable to move since he was still clenching her hair, she braced herself for the blow. . .but it never came. Instead, she watched as the arm in the air was wrenched backwards and twisted at an unnatural angle, so fast and quick that she heard a loud *pop* that indicat-

CARLY PHILLIPS & ERIKA WILDE

ed his shoulder had just been dislocated. With a scream of excruciating pain, Connor released her. When he whirled around, Katrina saw Mason, seconds before he slammed his fist into Connor's jaw with such force she heard another crack. Between the two consecutive blows, it took Connor off guard and knocked him onto his ass on the storeroom floor.

With his shoulder out of joint, he couldn't push himself up, but that didn't stop Mason from advancing on Connor.

"Goddamn motherfucker!" Mason yelled as he grabbed Connor by the shirt and hauled him back to his feet, shocking Katrina with his strength against a man who was military trained. But then again, Mason had never been afraid of anyone. He was lean and taut compared to Connor's bulk, and Mason had grown up a hot-tempered kid on the streets who'd learned to fight hard and dirty.

Connor winced and grabbed at his injured arm, his expression filled with a combination of pain and hostility as he glared at Mason. "What the hell, man?" he bit out angrily. "She came on to me, just like she did back in high school! I was just giving her what she wanted. She's a goddamn tramp!"

The lies he spewed no longer cut at Katrina as they once had. She stayed right where she was and kept quiet, because she knew Connor would deny anything she said in response. The only person who mattered, whom she needed to believe the truth, was Mason.

Mason shifted so he was standing in front of

Katrina—*protecting her*, she realized—but his gaze remained steady on Connor. "Just this once, I'm going to let you walk away with the rest of your limbs intact," Mason said in a low voice that belied just how enraged he still was. "But you so much as come near her again, in any way, shape, or form, and I will fucking annihilate you. I don't ever want to see your goddamn face again."

Connor's cut lip curled in one of those sneers as he glanced from Mason to Katrina. "Does he know that I've already had a piece of you? And way before he ever did," he said bitterly, clearly trying to disgrace her in front of Mason by making it sound as though she'd slept with him willingly.

When she said nothing, he returned his stare to Mason, his expression insolent. "Like I said the other night at the bar, she's a hot piece of ass."

Mason started toward Connor again, and Katrina grabbed his arm, stopping him before he pulverized the other guy and ended up getting arrested for assault. "Don't do it," she said softly, wanting all this to end. "He's not worth it."

Mason hesitated a moment, debating, then finally said, "Get the fuck out of my shop while you can still walk out."

With one last dirty look at both of them, Connor turned and walked out of the storeroom just as Jasmine arrived, her eyes huge as she took in the swelling already starting on Connor's face and the blood on his chin from where Katrina had bitten him. She quickly stepped back as Connor walked by.

"Oh, my God," Jasmine said as she rushed to Katrina. "What happened?"

Both Caleb and Derek arrived right then, too, the shock and concern on their faces telling Katrina that they'd also seen Connor on his way out.

"What the hell is going on?" Caleb asked, taking in the scene.

"That prick overstepped his boundaries, is all," Mason said gruffly. "If he sets foot in here again, call the police and have him arrested for trespassing."

Caleb nodded. "Jesus. Yeah. Of course."

"Give me a minute with Katrina?" Mason asked.

"Sure," Jasmine said, and the three of them left the storeroom.

Once they were gone, Mason turned around to face Katrina, his expression almost . . . agonized. "Are you okay?"

She nodded. "Yes." And it was true. Despite how things had just ended, being able to finally confront Connor felt oddly cleansing and cathartic. She felt lighter inside, as if she was no longer carrying around that huge burden that had ruled so much of her adult life.

Still frowning, Mason stepped up to her, slid his fingers beneath her chin, and lifted her face to check it thoroughly. "Did he hurt you?"

"No. You made sure of that." She didn't want to think of what might have happened if Mason hadn't arrived when he had.

"This time," he muttered, a thread of self-loathing in his voice. "Let's get out of here so we can talk, okay?"

Something was off with Mason, and Katrina couldn't deny that it worried her after everything Connor had said about her. "That's a good idea."

It was a conversation that was long overdue. Katrina just wished she could predict how it would all end once Mason knew the truth.

Chapter Fourteen

MASON WAS QUIET in the car, and when Katrina cast a surreptitious glance at his profile, it was obvious to her that he seemed troubled. His dark brows were furrowed into a frown, his jaw was clenched, and the thin line of his lips indicated that he was mulling over what had just happened back at Inked with Connor.

While she was relieved that she'd been able to face down those past demons once and for all, she couldn't deny that her nerves had kicked in again for a whole different reason. For the past three days, she'd pushed Mason away when he should have been the person she'd turned to. Between making him feel insignificant, then him being blindsided by all of Connor's lies, she honestly had no idea where they stood as a couple.

When he drove to her apartment, her heart filled with dread. Mason never bought her to her place if they were together, and she desperately tried not to read too deeply into the action.

He remained silent as he walked her to her door, then followed her inside. She set her purse on the small table in the entryway, headed into the living room, and sat down on the couch. Instead of joining her on the sofa, he paced restlessly back and forth in front of her, obviously too on edge to sit still.

He exhaled a deep breath and finally met her gaze, his blue eyes filled with a torment she didn't fully understand. "Is what Connor said true?" he asked, his voice raspy. "Back in high school, did he . . . "

He was waiting for her to finish the sentence, as if he knew that what had happened between her and Connor hadn't been consensual. "He raped me." There was no sugarcoating the truth.

He visibly shuddered and swore beneath his breath, his agony even more pronounced now. "Jesus, Katrina." He stared at her, his face etched with so much pain. "When?"

"Do you remember that huge party at Rick Ackerman's house when his parents were gone for the weekend? It was a few weeks before graduation, and you, me, and Connor went together." When he nodded, she folded her hands in her lap and went on, feeling calmer inside than she'd expected. "After you went off with Jessica later that night, Connor started making lewd advances and touching me inappropriately. He was drunk and obnoxious and I just wanted to get away from him. The downstairs bathroom was being used, so I went upstairs, and I didn't even know that he'd followed me until he pushed me into one of the empty bedrooms and locked us in. He was so much stronger than I was, and I just couldn't stop him no matter what I tried to do." She stopped there, knowing that Mason didn't need details.

"I'm so sorry." He dragged his hand down his face, his remorse a tangible thing. "I'm so fucking sorry."

She shook her head in confusion. "You have nothing to be sorry for, Mason. It wasn't your fault."

He didn't seem convinced. "I swore after what those bullies at the park did to you the day we met, and after learning about your stepfather's abuse, that I'd *always* protect you and keep you safe. And Jesus, I completely failed you when you needed me the most."

Mason's words shocked her. She'd been so worried that he'd look at her differently after discovering the truth. That it would change the dynamic of their relationship. Never would she have thought that he'd blame himself for something he hadn't had any control over.

She stood up and walked over to him, needing him to realize that he wasn't responsible for the actions of another man. "You didn't fail me," she said, looking directly into his dark blue eyes and hating the self-recrimination she saw there. "You didn't know what would happen that night, and there isn't anything you could have done to change the outcome. You need to believe that."

He let out a laugh that lacked any humor. "If I hadn't let my goddamn dick rule my brain back then, I would have been around you that night, and Connor never would have touched you." He cupped her face in his big hands, his touch so gentle and caring as he stared into her eyes. "You carried this around for eight years. Why didn't you tell me that night? The first thing you should have done was come and find me."

She managed a wry smile. "I think you were busy with Jessica," she said, trying to lighten things, because the truth was much harder to admit.

"I don't give a shit," he said vehemently. "You are the single most important thing in my life, Katrina. There never has been, and never will be, another woman who will ever matter more to me than you do. Ever. Why would you doubt that I wouldn't be there for you? That I'd do everything in my power to make sure that something like that would never happen again?"

"Once it was over, there wasn't anything you could have done to change that fact." Knowing the rest of her explanation was more difficult for her to say, she tried to turn her head to the side so she didn't have to look directly into his eyes, but he wouldn't allow her to retreat from him in any way. "After Conner assaulted me, I was ashamed and humiliated and I felt so . . . dirty. And he told me that if I said anything to you, he'd just say that I came on to him, that I wanted it, just like he did today."

"And you honestly thought I'd believe him?" Mason asked incredulously.

She didn't miss the hurt in his tone. "I was only seventeen at the time, and I kept thinking about what had happened with Owen, and how my mom didn't believe me when I told her that he was touching me inappropriately. And how Owen turned everything around and blamed me for being a slut, and that my mother chose to side with a man she barely knew, over her own daughter."

His gaze softened in understanding as his thumbs tenderly glided along her cheeks. "I get it."

But there was more she needed to tell him. "I was also afraid that after Connor's attack, if you knew what happened, that you'd look at me differently. That you'd treat me differently. And I never wanted it to change our friendship."

"Oh, Kitty-Kat," he said softly as he drew her into his arms and hugged her tight. "I had an uneasy feeling about Connor after a conversation we had at Kincaid's the other night, and I should have listened to my gut then and told him to fuck off."

Katrina burrowed closer against Mason's warm, strong body and laid her head on his chest. "No more regrets or blame, okay, Mason? I don't want to live in the past anymore."

"Okay," he agreed as he wrapped one arm around her waist and slid the fingers of his other hand into her hair and gently massaged her scalp. "As long as you promise that you won't ever keep secrets like this from me again."

She closed her eyes and breathed in the warm, masculine scent of him. "I promise."

"There's one more thing I need you to be honest about," he said after a long moment had passed. "The scars on your hip . . . you said it was a relapse. Did it happen after that night with Connor?"

She swallowed hard. No more secrets; she'd promised him. "Yes."

He swore succinctly, and when he squeezed those muscular arms tighter around her, she knew that he was internalizing her response.

"No more regrets or blame," she reminded him. "It's done and in the past. The only things I want to think about are the future and us." *Hopefully, you still want that, too.*

"About the future and us . . . " He gently eased her away so that he was looking down at her face, his eyes suddenly very serious. "We need to talk about that."

She had no idea where this conversation was headed, or where it would end. Her biggest fear was that her behavior over the past three days had pushed him too far away and changed everything between them, or he'd come to the conclusion that he didn't want to be tied down to one woman. She'd always known that was a possibility.

"I've been thinking a lot about us," he started out tentatively, which only increased her sudden bout of nerves. "You know my past. You know I grew up without real parents and had a mother who was an addict and prostitute, then went to prison and left all three of us boys with an abusive prick. And even though Clay raised me and put up with all my crap, I always felt unworthy of being loved. I thought I wasn't good enough for anyone *to* love. It was easier to push people away than let them close and risk any kind of rejection. And because of that, I just fell into an easy, no-commitment pattern with women because it was safe and uncomplicated."

He paused for a moment, and Katrina waited patiently, knowing that whatever he had to say was difficult for him, because he wasn't the type of guy to talk about emotional stuff.

Exhaling a deep breath, he slid his hands down her arms until he was holding her hands. "But from the very beginning, you were different, and you were the first girl I ever shared anything with. You knew my past. You knew my secrets. No matter what I did, and I certainly wasn't a choirboy as a teenager or as an adult, you never judged me. You never left me, even though there were times that I knew I did some stupid shit that should have had you questioning why you were friends with me. You were always *there*."

She swallowed the knot of uncertainty in her throat and forced a smile. "That's what best friends are for, right?"

"You will always be my best friend, Kitty-Kat," he said with a gentle smile she couldn't completely read. "And I've *always* loved you, which is why it was so easy to fall *in love* with you over these past few weeks together. And this weekend, when you started to pull away and withdraw, it scared the shit out of me. The thought of losing you, in any way, changed everything for me and put things into perspective, too."

Her mind was still stuck on the *it was so easy to fall in love with you* part of his statement, but soon caught up with the rest. "How so?" she asked, her voice a whisper of hope as her heart fluttered in her chest.

"I want you in my life *forever*," he said, without an ounce of doubt in his deep, masculine voice. "Every morning and every night. As my best friend. As my perfect lover. As my beautiful wife."

Certain she'd misheard that last part, her eyes grew round with disbelief. "Your . . . your *wife*?"

"I'm so in love with you, Katrina, and if I marry you, that makes you mine *forever*." Then, a boyish smile curved the corner of his mouth, and his eyes glimmered playfully. "Umm, that is, if you want to be mine forever. I guess I shouldn't assume anything."

She bit her lip as tears of happiness filled her eyes. "Yes, I want to be yours forever. I love you, Mason Kincaid. I've loved you since the day you rescued me from those bullies. I was just waiting and hoping that someday you'd feel the same way."

"I'm such an idiot. It took me long enough," he said, and finally kissed her, slow, hot, and deep.

The hunger and desire didn't take long to become a raging need that neither one of them could deny. He skimmed his hands down her back and over her bottom, then gripped her thighs and guided her legs around his waist. Once she had her ankles locked tight at the base of his spine, he walked to her bedroom, and didn't break the kiss until they were next to her bed and her heels were steady on the floor again.

When he finally lifted his mouth from hers, he grinned down at her. "Best thing I ever did was carry you out of Coyote Ugly that night and get into your pants. You were so fucking sexy and hot that my dick decided right then and there that you were the only woman he would ever get hard for, which is more than fine by me."

She laughed happily as she pushed up his T-shirt and pulled it over his head and off. "I'll keep him very happy, I promise."

When she reached for the button on his jeans, he caught her wrists and stopped her, his intense gaze going serious once again. "So, back to that forever thing we just talked about?"

She tipped her head to the side. "Yes?"

"That's where I was this morning," he said, and now he looked adorably nervous. "I met up with Samantha so she could help me take care of the forever part of our relationship."

Katrina couldn't be more confused. "I'm not sure what that means."

Releasing her hands, he pushed his fingers into the front pocket of his jeans. He pulled out a condom and grinned sheepishly at her. "Umm, wrong pocket, but yeah, I was hopeful that I'd get lucky today." He tossed the foil packet onto the bed, then reached into the other side and this time withdrew a small black velvet box.

Everything inside of Katrina went still, and she could barely breathe as he opened the lid and revealed a stunning ring that was set with a continuous line of round, brilliant diamonds. She was shocked and speechless.

He removed the sparkling band, picked up her left hand, and put it on her ring finger. "I needed Samantha's help to pick out the perfect ring for you. It's called an eternity band, and that's how long I'm going to love you. For an eternity."

So much emotion tightened her throat, and her heart filled with joy as she looked from the ring circling her finger back to Mason. "That's a really long time."

"I know. I'm in it for the long haul." Smiling warmly at her, he gently brushed his fingers along her cheek, then walked behind her to unzip her dress. "One more thing before I lay you back on that bed and make you mine. Do you know why I brought you here to your apartment instead of my house?"

She shook her head, remembering her earlier thoughts when they'd arrived here. "No. Why?"

Done opening her dress, he pushed the sleeves down her arms, and the outfit slid down her body and fell to the floor at her feet. He placed a warm, damp kiss on her bare shoulder as he unfastened her strapless bra and let that drop to the ground, too. Cool air touched her breasts and her nipples tightened into hard, aching points.

"Because after I get my fill of you, which might take a long while, we are packing up all your stuff and taking it to my place," he said as he hooked his fingers into the waistband of her panties and eased them down her thighs until they joined the rest of her clothing. "You're not staying in this apartment ever again. After today, you will be in my bed every single night. Do you understand?"

The slightest bit of authority in his voice made her shift anxiously on her heels, and she moaned when he followed up that statement with a light, playful smack to her ass. "Yes, I understand," she said, wanting the same thing.

"Good. Now take off your shoes and get up on the bed," he ordered, knowing how much it turned her on when he got bossy. "I want to fuck you wearing nothing but that ring on your finger."

She did as he asked, and by the time she was settled, he'd stripped off the rest of his clothes and was as naked as she was. He was so gorgeous, from his masculine features to those tattoos she loved, to his toned chest, lean abs, and that thick, hard cock between his legs. *And he was all hers*, she thought giddily.

He sheathed his erect shaft and climbed up on the bed between her spread legs, and starting at her knee, he slowly, lazily kissed his way up her thighs, until they quivered with anticipation and she was panting with need. His wicked mouth and tongue lingered at her core, licking and sliding through her sensitive folds of flesh. Over. And over. And over.

When she was beyond wet and aroused, he moved on, detouring to the scars on her hip. He kissed each one lovingly, replacing the reasons they were there with the pleasure of his touch. He teased her nipples next, sliding his tongue over them, nipping at them with his teeth, then sucking those engorged tips deep into his mouth until she was desperate for the orgasm he'd so reverently built to a peak but withheld just out of her reach. When she couldn't stand the sensual torment any longer, she finally reached down, twisted her fingers in his hair, and brought his lips up to hers.

The kiss was as hot and deep as the single thrust of his shaft driving into her. She gasped and undulated her hips, causing him to groan, low and harsh. He lifted his head and stared down at her, the emotion in his gaze filling her heart to overflowing for this man. Her best friend. Her lover. And soon, her husband.

"You're mine, Kitty-Kat," he said possessively as he threaded their fingers together and pinned her hands above her head before he started to move, claiming her in the most intimate way possible. "Forever."

"Yes," she whispered back, knowing she'd never get tired of hearing that. "Yours. Forever."

Everything about being with Mason felt incredible. His powerful body. The sensual passion between them. The need. And the love.

Especially that. And it was all hers, for an eternity.

✧   ✧   ✧

"JUST A LITTLE bit longer and I'll be done," Mason said. "You doing okay?"

Katrina lay on her side on the padded table in Mason's station at Inked while he finished up her newest tattoo. It was after hours, and they were alone in the shop, and while the pain was noticeable considering how large the design was, she was handling the process pretty well. Meditating had definitely helped to take the edge off the worst part of the discomfort.

"I'm good," she said, anxious to see the finished piece, which she'd created herself. And this time, it was fitting that Mason was the one to cover the scars on her hip. He was the one who'd helped her recover emotionally, and this was her way of moving on from all the pain lingering in her past. Now when she looked in the mirror, instead of those hideous cuts and slices that were a part of a life she no longer lived, she'd now see a beautiful cluster of butterflies, to match the ones on her arm.

The past few months living with Mason had been amazing. She'd never been so happy, so content or at peace with herself. She knew Mason felt the same with his own emotions and with her. They were two damaged people who'd managed to heal each other with something as simple as unconditional love. The fact that they were best friends who had phenomenal sex was a bonus.

She moved the hand on the table, and the lights glinted off her eternity band, making her smile when she remembered the day he'd put it on her finger.

They'd talked about marriage, and she was more than ready to take that next step with Mason. He'd assured her that he was ready to make that final commitment, as well, and told her to make whatever plans she wanted, and he'd show up wherever and whenever she told him to. *Typical man*, she thought.

But he was *her* man, and after fourteen years of unrequited love, it felt damn good to be the only woman he wanted. The only woman he'd ever loved.

She felt him wipe away the last of the ink and watched as he put his tattoo machine down. "Ready to see what it looks like?" he asked.

She nodded, and he helped her down from the table. They walked over to the full-length mirror, and she looked at the reflection of her design that Mason had brought to life. The colorful butterflies were stunning. What was once so ugly and made her feel shame and humiliation was now pretty and captivating and made her feel beautiful.

Overwhelming emotion crowded in her throat and happy tears filled her eyes. "It's gorgeous," she whispered in awe as she met Mason's warm gaze. "You did an amazing job. I can't even see where the scars are anymore. Thank you."

"You're welcome and it was my absolute pleasure to lay that ink on your skin." He curled his fingers around the back of her head and pulled her to him so he could drop a sweet kiss on her temple. "However, I have to confess that I took some creative liberty with the design."

"You did?" She glanced back into the mirror, scrutinizing the butterflies a bit longer and harder this time, but couldn't find anything that stood out. "What did you do?"

"It's right here," he said, and pointed to one of the butterflies' wings, his expression a bit smug. "I made the veins into a word that I think you'll like."

She looked closer, and then she saw it, the word *mine* integrated into the lines crisscrossing one of the wings. His modification wasn't obvious unless you were specifically looking for it, and it blended in naturally. But she loved that it was there, and that just the two of them were privy to the secret.

She grinned at him. "Possessive much?" she teased.

"With you? Always." He wrapped an arm around her waist and brought her body flush to his as his hand grabbed her ass. "Though I don't expect anyone to get up close and personal with that tattoo except for me, considering where it's placed."

He moved his hips against hers, and Katrina's eyes widened in shock. "Oh, my God!" she said as she felt his erection grind against her lower belly. "Are you seriously *hard*?"

"I can't help it," he said with an unrepentant laugh that held sinful undertones. "Seeing my ink on you is such a fucking turn-on. Kinda brings out the inner caveman in me and makes me want to conquer and claim."

"Well, who am I to interfere with your need to play

the Neanderthal?" she said as she rose up on her toes and kissed his lips. After all, she was his, in ink and in truth. Forever.

Next up: Levi Kincaid –
Get **DIRTY SEXY CUFFED** Today!

Thank you for reading DIRTY SEXY INKED. We would appreciate it if you would help others enjoy this book too. Please recommend to others and leave a review.

Sign up for Carly Phillips & Erika Wilde's Newsletters:

Carly's Newsletter
http://smarturl.it/CarlysNewsletter

Erika's Newsletter
http://smarturl.it/ErikaWildeNewsletter

Dirty Sexy Series Reading Order:
Dirty Sexy Saint (Clay Kincaid)
Dirty Sexy Inked (Mason Kincaid)
Dirty Sexy Cuffed (Levi Kincaid)
*Every book in the Dirty Sexy series can be read alone for your reading enjoyment!

Read on for Excerpts of Carly & Erika's books:
DARE TO SURRENDER by Carly Phillips
PLAYING WITH TEMPTATION by Erika Wilde

Dare to Surrender

Excerpt

by Carly Phillips

G ABRIEL DARE EYED the beautiful woman with the bright smile that didn't reach her eyes, hoping his bland expression concealed the intense emotions she roused inside him. Protective instincts the likes of which he'd never experienced before. The desire to sweep her into his arms, breathe in her unique scent no designer could have created, and steal her away from this god-awful staid country club was strong.

He had an endless supply of beautiful women all eager to share his bed, including Naomi, his latest affair, and yet they did nothing for him except accompany him on endless nights like this one. And take the edge off his need. True satisfaction hadn't existed for him in far too long.

He was bored. Unless he was watching *her*. Then the perfection and elegance of the Hamptons club vanished, and *she* was all he saw.

Blonde hair fell down her back in less-than-perfect waves, defying the stick-straight look most women preferred. Her lush, sexy body, so unlike the females he normally bedded, had his hands itching to learn those curves and show her what true pleasure really was. She was unattainable, living with one of Wall Street's stars, but she could do so much better.

Oddly, it wasn't her lack of availability that appealed. She was bright, witty, and she could hold her own with just about anyone, making whoever she spoke to feel important. He admired that trait. They hadn't spent more than a few minutes here and there in each other's company, but she'd taken his breath away from the first look.

Gabe would do just about anything to attain something he wanted, but he drew the line at poaching on another man's territory. Still, he had to admit she tested even his willpower, and he'd had practice at being alone. He'd married young and miscalculated badly. Afterwards, he'd been certain that after Krissie's death, for which he felt responsible, the smart thing would be to keep a safe emotional distance from women.

One look at Isabelle Masters and he'd changed his mind. There was something about her that filled the emptiness inside him. To the point where just watching her was enough to calm his usually restless soul. Unfortunately, they didn't run into each other nearly often enough.

Gabe ran a hand through his hair, groaning as he caught sight of Naomi making her way toward him, a cocktail plate with one celery stick and a carrot in her hand. His gaze darted to Isabelle as she crossed the room in the opposite direction, careful to avoid him as long as the man she lived with was around.

She was taken, and all he could do was admire. Look and not touch. But if she ever became available, all bets were off.

Start Reading Dare to Surrender NOW!

Playing with Temptation
Excerpt

by Erika Wilde

R AINA BECK FINISHED helping a customer select a
bottle of warming massage oil, then headed over
to the lingerie section of her store, Sugar and Spice, a
sensual, upscale adult boutique that catered to the
residents of San Diego. She paused at the rack of new
arrivals, where her good friend, Jillian Noble, was
perusing the gorgeous items.

"Find anything you like?" Raina asked as the other
woman contemplated a leopard-print bustier before
putting it back on the stand.

Jillian smiled at her as she shuffled through a few
more pieces. "The problem is, there's too much to
like, which is a good thing. I'm looking for something
a little different than everything I already have…" Her
words trailed off, and her eyes lit up as she lifted a
hanger displaying a sexy red ensemble that consisted
of a demi bra, a short flirty skirt that was only a few
inches of fabric that would barely cover her bottom,
and a matching lace thong, along with a garter belt and
thigh-high stockings.

"I think this is it," Jillian announced with a succinct nod of her head.

"If Dean comes home to find you wearing that outfit, I think all bets are off," Raina teased her friend.

"That's what I'm counting on, and I think he'll really like the short little skirt, too." She handed the hanger to Raina. "I'll take it, along with one of those feather ticklers you have on display, the one with the soft ostrich feathers."

"You got it." Raina smiled, knowing Jillian, a good customer, appreciated the more sexually adventurous items Sugar and Spice provided to those who wanted to kink up their sex lives. Selecting a tickler with deep red feathers to match the outfit, she met her friend up at the front counter.

As she rang up Jillian's purchases, she asked, "How are you enjoying working with Stephanie?"

"I absolutely love it. I couldn't be happier," Jillian said, her expression reflecting her newfound joy. "I'm helping her design those fantasy suites at the hotel, and tomorrow I have a consultation with a woman who wants to redecorate her bedroom in a sexier version theme of The Secret Garden theme."

"Sounds like a fun project." Raina swiped Jillian's credit card to process the sale. The two of them had become close friends over the past months, and because she knew Jillian's husband had been so opposed to his wife taking a job, Raina couldn't help but wonder how that was going. "Is everything still good with Dean and you working for Stephanie?"

"He's getting used to it and adjusting. I make sure I always make time for just the two of us, and it keeps him happy."

"Men really are such basic creatures," Raina said with a laugh. "Keep them plied with food and sex and they're happy, content, and satisfied."

Jillian lifted a curious brow. "Speaking of men and sex…when are *you* going to indulge a little?"

Raina shrugged as she wrapped her ensemble in pink tissue and tucked it into a bag. "I think all the good guys are taken. And then there's the men who find out I own a sex toy boutique and decide I'm fair game for outrageous, kinky sex, because, you know, I have access to all sorts of depraved items."

She rolled her eyes to make light of her comment, but the truth ran much deeper and stirred up other painful memories that reminded her of why she kept her heart and emotions under lock and key—the pain of such complete and utter rejection was something that had left her guarded and very cautious when it came to a man's interest in her.

Admittedly, she *did* enjoy hot, adventurous sex. After all, she'd opened Sugar and Spice as a way to help women empower themselves sexually, to get in touch with their desires and be confident enough to enjoy every aspect of sex. But she also knew it took an equally strong, self-assured man to accept her line of business, to not feel threatened or embarrassed by the fact that she owned a boutique that catered to enhancing sexual pleasure.

Unfortunately, over the years, she'd learned that she wasn't the best judge of character when it came to a man's motives and his reasons for dating her, which also made it extremely difficult to decipher what was *real*, or if she was nothing more than someone's dirty little secret that he used until the excitement wore off.

Too many painful experiences had taught her that because of what she did for a living, men were more than willing to fuck her like a porn star in private, but they drew the line at taking her out in public or bringing her home to meet the family, which made her feel cheap and dirty—as if her own father's fire and brimstone prediction about her being a whore had come true. Men didn't date *a woman like her* with long term in mind, and it had become much easier for Raina to keep her emotional distance rather than face criticism and the sting of rejection all over again.

She'd been burned a few times, and she wasn't allowing any man to get close enough to do it again. Now, sex was all about physical pleasure, nothing more, and she'd recently decided that if anyone was going to do the *using*, it was going to be *her* for a change. Unfortunately, an opportunity hadn't presented itself, but if the right guy came along, she certainly wasn't opposed to enjoying a no-strings-attached one-night stand.

"Maybe you need hot *anonymous* sex," Jillian suggested with a naughty twinkle in her eye, as if she'd had a direct link to Raina's thoughts.

"It's been a long dry spell and the idea is definitely

tempting," Raina replied, a humorous note lacing the truth of her words. Vibrators and sex toys did the job as far as getting her off, but they couldn't replace the feel or pleasure of a strong, powerful, virile man thrusting deep inside of her or skimming his hands along her curves, his hot mouth seducing hers.

Yes, she definitely missed that, and the provocative thought made her feel a bit flushed.

Jillian bit her bottom lip for a second before reaching into her purse and pulling out a white envelope. "You've done a lot for me, and I want to do something for you for a change. Take this, and indulge yourself." She pushed the envelope across the counter to Raina.

Raina picked it up and read the word *Welcome* embossed in black across the front. "What is this?" she asked, confused and curious at the same time.

"An invitation to The Players Club."

Raina's eyes widened in surprise, and her heart fluttered in her chest with undeniable excitement. She knew exactly what The Players Club was—a private, members-only sex club that catered to an elite and prominent clientele in order to maintain its exclusivity. A personal recommendation was required to even visit the club, and since Dean and Jillian had recently become members, they now had the privilege of extending an invitation to a guest.

And Jillian had chosen *her*.

"Oh, wow," Raina breathed as she brushed her thumb over the embossed lettering on the envelope, still in shock. "Really?"

"Yes, *really*," Jillian mimicked playfully. "You deserve a sexy night all to yourself, and I can guarantee that *any* fantasy you have can be fulfilled at The Players Club."

Raina had plenty of private, naughty fantasies stored away in the deepest recesses of her mind, none of which she'd ever shared because those scenarios were just too wicked and forbidden to reveal to any of the guys she'd dated up to this point, all of whom had big egos and had been self-centered lovers. Yes, she owned a boutique that sold all sorts of kinky items to enhance sex play, but it took a strong, confident man who didn't feel threatened by her expertise to give her what she desired, who knew what she needed without asking and made that pleasure his sole focus.

Finding that kind of compelling man at The Players Club in one night was improbable but certainly more possible than in her daily life, and she wasn't about to refuse Jillian's gift. She'd been given the equivalent of Willy Wonka's golden ticket, but instead of gorging on chocolate, she planned to indulge in as many orgasms as she could.

Start Reading Playing with Temptation NOW!

About the Authors

Carly Phillips

Carly Phillips is the *N.Y. Times* and *USA Today* Best-selling Author of over 50 sexy contemporary romance novels featuring hot men, strong women and the emotionally compelling stories her readers have come to expect and love. Carly is happily married to her college sweetheart, the mother of two nearly adult daughters and three crazy dogs (two wheaten terriers and one mutant Havanese) who star on her Facebook Fan Page and website. Carly loves social media and is always around to interact with her readers. You can find out more about Carly at www.carlyphillips.com.

Erika Wilde

Erika Wilde is the author of the sexy Marriage Diaries series and The Players Club series. She lives in Oregon with her husband and two daughters, and when she's not writing you can find her exploring the beautiful Pacific Northwest. For more information on her upcoming releases, please visit website at www. erikawilde.com.